"Are you coming?"

Matt turned to face Olivia, a look of exasperation in his eyes. "Or are you determined to make this more difficult than it already is?"

Olivia caught her breath. "More difficult?" she echoed, aware that he could misinterpret the indignation in her tone. But it wasn't fair that he should pass judgments about her. He had no idea how painful this all was.

"I didn't ask you to come," she exclaimed, taking refuge in the childish retort.

"No." Matt sighed after a moment. "You didn't ask me to come. And you're making it bloody plain you wish I hadn't." Then he added wearily, "But please don't make a scene here! I'm prepared to forget the past and so should you. Ten years is too long for me to bear a grudge— or for you to feel a sense of guilt!"

ANNE MATHER began her career by writing the kind of book she likes to read—romance. Married, with two children, this northern England author has become a favorite with readers of romance fiction the world over—her books have been translated into many languages and are read in countless countries. Since her first novel was published in 1970, Anne Mather has written more than eighty romances, with over ninety million copies sold!

Books by Anne Mather

STORMSPELL
WILD CONCERTO
HIDDEN IN THE FLAME
THE LONGEST PLEASURE

HARLEQUIN PRESENTS

1210—DARK MOSAIC
1251—A FEVER IN THE BLOOD
1315—A RELATIVE BETRAYAL
1354—INDISCRETION
1444—BLIND PASSION
1458—SUCH SWEET POISON

HARLEQUIN ROMANCE

1631—MASQUERADE
1656—AUTUMN OF THE WITCH

ANNE MATHER

Betrayed

Harlequin Books

TORONTO • NEW YORK • LONDON
AMSTERDAM • PARIS • SYDNEY • HAMBURG
STOCKHOLM • ATHENS • TOKYO • MILAN
MADRID • WARSAW • BUDAPEST • AUCKLAND

Harlequin Presents first edition September 1992
ISBN 0-373-11492-3

Original hardcover edition published in 1991
by Mills & Boon Limited

BETRAYED

CHAPTER ONE

THE aircraft banked over the Thames, and the sun, which had been dazzling Olivia's eyes moments before, swung across the cabin to blind the passengers sitting on the other side. Below her, the sprawling mass of London and its suburbs was giving way to the more sparsely populated area around the airport, and she heard the grinding rush of the undercarriage being activated as the huge jet made its final approach to Heathrow.

Her stomach flipped, but not because of the excitement of landing. At least, not with any feeling of anticipation, she acknowledged tensely. Rather, it was the awareness that in a matter of minutes she would be setting foot on British soil again, something she had believed she would never do.

Of course, when she had made that vow to herself she had been more than ten years younger, she reflected drily, remembering the devastation she had felt when she was leaving. Her whole world had been falling apart—or that was the way it had seemed then. She had been desperate to get away, desperate to put as many miles between her and Lower Mychett as was humanly possible. She doubted even her grandmother had expected quite such a violent reaction, but then, Harriet Stoner was not one to regret her words. And, to be fair, she had discovered that at least a part of what her grandmother had told her was true; time did effect change; and what had once seemed a justifiable reason for cutting herself off from the rest of her family no longer seemed so important.

Or did it?

Impatiently, Olivia ran her fingers into the crimped mass of streaked blonde hair that brushed her shoulders at the sides and dipped slightly longer in the back. Wasn't that part of the reason why she had come back, after all? she pondered, resting her hands at the back of her neck. Oh, her grandmother's death should be reason enough, she supposed, but it had been ten years since she had seen her, and they had never been particularly close. On the contrary, the old lady had never made any secret of the fact that she favoured Olivia's younger brother and sister, and her eventual revelations had only confirmed the reason for her dislike.

Still, when her mother's telegraphed message had arrived, Olivia had hardly hesitated before booking her flight to England. In spite of all that had gone before, she had decided to attend the funeral, and not even Perry's unconcealed disapproval could sway her from her purpose. Perhaps this was what she had been waiting for, she thought consideringly. Perhaps she needed this visit—this purging of the spirit, almost—before she could truly settle down to living the rest of her life in the United States. Goodness knew, she had been vacillating over her relationship with Perry for months now, and sooner or later she was going to have to make a decision. She loved him—of course she did—but she had told herself she wasn't entirely convinced that she wanted to give up her independence just yet. Now, however, she wondered whether she hadn't unconsciously been waiting for something—or someone—to make up her mind for her. This trip to England, to the village of Lower Mychett in Hampshire, where she had been born, would prove to her once and for all that the past was dead. Like her grandmother, she reflected bitterly. She just wished she could feel a sense of pity.

But it was difficult to feel anything for the woman who had so dispassionately devastated her young life. At eighteen she had been on the brink of what she had believed would be a wonderful future, and to have it all taken away had been the cruellest kind of torture. It had all sounded so melodramatic, after all. One of those awful family affairs you read about in the newspapers, but never expected to experience. At first she hadn't be-

lieved it. She knew her grandmother had always re-
sented her, and Olivia had half convinced herself that
the old lady was just making it up to hurt her. But she
wasn't. The letters had proved that. And when Olivia
had realised that she and Matthew were——

She supposed she ought to have blamed her mother,
not her grandmother, but she hadn't. How could she
have blamed her mother for anything? Ever since Olivia's
younger sister, Sara, was born, Felicity Stoner had suffered from a heart condition and, in consequence, she
was indulged by every member of the family, including
her besotted husband. The idea of Olivia accusing her
mother of ruining her life didn't bear thinking about.
Besides, it would have meant telling her father, too, and
her grandmother had impressed upon her the fact that
Robert Stoner knew nothing.

Olivia sighed, tipping her head back against her hands
and stretching the slender column of her throat. The
action unknowingly caused her breasts to press against
the silky fabric of her shirt, and the man sitting next to
her observed the movement with undisguised approval.

'Nervous?' he enquired hopefully, and Olivia, who had
spent the early part of the journey fending off his unwanted attentions, shook her head.

'No.'

'Ah.' The man, who was possibly in his late thirties,
and evidently convinced of his own attractions, patently
didn't believe her. 'Well, don't worry. I cross the Atlantic
at least half a dozen times every month, and landing one
of these things is a piece of cake.'

'You're a pilot?' enquired Olivia politely, deciding that
as they were preparing to land she had nothing to lose,
and the man's pale, plump features took on a faint trace
of colour.

'I didn't say that,' he replied, a little tersely, and
Olivia's lips twisted as she turned to the window to watch
their descent. 'I just meant my business takes me to the
States fairly frequently, and I feel quite at home in a
747.'

'Really?'

Olivia tried to keep the impatience out of her voice, without really succeeding. But honestly, some men, seeing a woman travelling alone, couldn't help but regard her as a challenge. She had hoped that travelling first class—Perry's idea—would have alleviated that phenomenon, but it hadn't worked that way. Still, she supposed it wasn't his fault that her nerves were on edge, and that indulging in small talk only made her feel worse, not better.

'Oh, yes,' her companion went on now, proving that his skin was just as thick as she had anticipated. 'I guess you could say I'm a seasoned traveller. A paid-up member of the mile-high club.' His blue eyes narrowed assessingly. 'Do you know what I mean?'

Olivia's patience ran out. 'That you like playing doctor in the lavatory?' she suggested coolly, watching the heat surge into his cheeks, and his mouth take on an aggressive curve.

'Clever bitch!' he muttered, shifting irritably inside his seatbelt, and Olivia turned her attention back to the window, wishing the journey were over.

The wheels touched the runway only seconds later, and the high-powered whine of the reverse thrust briefly silenced the anxious clamour in her head. But the sudden conviction that she shouldn't have come was borne in on her as the jet's engines pushed her back against the cushions of her seat, and she closed her eyes.

What was she trying to prove, after all? That she hadn't lost touch with her family? Of course she had! In spite of her many invitations, her parents had never made the trip to New York to see her. And although she had told herself it was because they were country people, and that the idea of travelling across the Atlantic was too adventurous for them, she knew in her heart of hearts that that wasn't the real reason. The fact was, her father, at least, had never forgiven her for leaving home, and without the right to tell him the truth she had damned herself forever in his eyes.

Maybe she wanted to prove to herself that leaving Lower Mychett had been the best thing she had ever done. Surely that was true? Staying would only have made the whole situation even more painful than it already was, and Olivia knew she hadn't had that kind of strength. Besides, her grandmother had encouraged her to make a clean break, and there hadn't seemed any other way of doing it.

Perhaps her real reason for making this journey was to assure herself that Harriet Stoner was really dead, she considered bitterly. But even she was not that vindictive. After all, her grandmother had had her best interests at heart, even if it hadn't seemed so at the time.

She opened her eyes, as the plane taxied towards its unloading bay, and the steward began handing out coats and jackets to the waiting passengers. And for the first time she allowed herself to wonder whether she didn't secretly hope that she might see Matthew again. It wasn't that the memory of what she had once felt for him was anything more than a rather foolish aberration. Given the way she felt now, she guessed she would have got over her infatuation for him in her own time, if her grandmother had not chosen to interfere. But Harriet Stoner had not been prepared to take the risk, and who could blame her? Her daughter-in-law had turned a blind eye to what was going on, but she couldn't. She was a God-fearing woman, a stalwart of the church, and her strict moral values would not allow her to keep silent.

Olivia's lips trembled for a moment, as she remembered how horrified she had felt then. At eighteen, everything had seemed so much more clearly defined; things were either black or white, with no room for shades of grey. Now, she knew different. Her experiences in New York had taught her that life was an ever-changing kaleidoscope of colours, and what had shocked her ten years ago would now barely warrant a lifting of her eyebrows. In New York, at least, she amended, loosening her safety-belt. No doubt in Lower Mychett the stigma would still remain.

The enclosed gangway had been secured to the aircraft's side now, and the heavy door was swung open. Her fellow passengers crowded round the crew, wanting to be the first to reach Immigration, and to her relief the man beside her left without a backward glance. Sliding her arms into the sleeves of her jacket, Olivia gathered her handbag and the Louis Vuitton travel bag Perry had bought her, and got reluctantly to her feet.

'Are you feeling all right, Miss Stoner?'

One of the stewardesses was at her elbow, and Olivia gave her a fleeting smile. 'Yes. I'm fine, thank you.'

'I just thought——' The stewardess hesitated. 'You seemed rather reluctant to leave.'

'Perhaps I am,' remarked Olivia ruefully. And then, seeing the doubt in the other woman's eyes, she shook her head. 'No. I was just dawdling, that's all. Thank you.'

The walk to Immigration was invigorating. At this hour of the morning the airport corridors were cool and uncrowded, and Olivia enjoyed stretching her long legs. Seven hours in a plane was too long, she acknowledged, shifting her travel bag to her other hand. But she had resisted Perry's efforts to send her on Concorde. Perhaps even then she had been subconsciously delaying the moment when she would have to meet her family again.

By the time she had cleared Passport Control and collected her suitcase, it was nearly nine o'clock. She had sent an answering cable to her mother, saying she would be arriving today, but she didn't expect anyone to meet her. For one thing, it was harvest time, and as both her father and her brother worked on the Rycroft estate they would have little time to spare for a trip to London, especially to meet the apparent black sheep of the family.

There were few porters about, and, loading her suitcase and travel bag on to a trolley, Olivia looped her bag over her shoulder, and set off to run the gamut of Customs. She chose the green channel. She had nothing to declare, and she emerged unscathed into the noisy Arrivals hall.

There were at least a hundred people thronged around the Arrivals gate. Some stared at her curiously, as if trying to decide if she was someone of importance, while others held up placards announcing their identity to the incoming passengers. But none of the placards held her name, and she was not surprised when she reached the end of the enclosure undeterred.

And yet, she must have thought someone *might* come to meet her, she reflected wryly, for she had refused to let Perry make any ongoing arrangements for the trip to Lower Mychett. She could take a taxi into London, of course, and find out the times of trains to Winchester. But the idea of facing the M4 in the rush hour—which was probably twice as bad now as it had been when she went away—was not appealing. Matthew used to meet her in London, she remembered fleetingly, and take her to his room at the college, but she thrust the thought away...

Perhaps she could hire a car, she thought determinedly. She had a driving licence, and although it had been obtained in the United States there were plenty of Americans who came to England for fly-drive holidays. Even so, she suspected they made their arrangements well in advance. Did she need an international driving licence, for example, and, if so, where could she get one? *Could* she get one? Probably not soon enough to get her to Lower Mychett for her grandmother's funeral, she decided wearily. Oh, why hadn't she let Perry arrange a hire car for her?

Because she *had* thought someone would meet her, she reminded herself again. After all, the letters she infrequently exchanged with her mother maintained the fiction of their relationship, so why shouldn't she have asked her brother or her sister to meet her?

'Olivia.'

The sound of her name scraped over nerves bared by her confusion, and Olivia swung round to face the speaker in utter disbelief. 'M-Matthew!'

'Hi.' He inclined his head in a gesture of acknowl-edgement. 'How are you?'

'Um—fine. I'm fine.' Olivia swallowed, and glanced uneasily about her. 'Did—um——' She frowned. 'Did you come to meet me?'

'Well, I'm not plane-spotting,' responded Matthew drily, his lean, dark features a bland impassive mask. 'Did you have a good trip?'

Olivia expelled her breath in a rush. This couldn't be happening, she decided unsteadily. Somehow she had conjured up Matthew's image, and this conversation—this unnaturally *polite* conversation—was just a figment of her imagination. Dear God, when she remembered how he had reacted when she had told him of her plans to go to the United States. He had been furious—no, *incensed.* She had half thought he was going to hit her, and the words he had used to describe her were forever imprinted on her memory. That was why this little scenario had to be a hallucination. The Matthew she re-membered would never have forgiven her. Of course, she hadn't been able to tell him the truth either, she thought bitterly. And in the same position she guessed she would have felt the same, if Matthew had walked out on her. After all, they had been in love. *In love!* Oh, God...

'Is this all your luggage?' Matthew was asking now, and Olivia dragged her thoughts back to the present.

'What?' She stared at him blankly. And then, re-alising what he had said, she nodded jerkily. 'Oh—yes. Yes. This is all.'

She looked about her as she spoke, half expecting to find herself the object of a dozen curious eyes, but no one was staring at her—not as if she was mad, anyway, she amended—so, if she was talking to herself, no one had noticed.

'Are you all right?'

It was the second time someone had asked her that in the space of an hour, and Olivia forced herself to look

at him again. 'Yes,' she said. 'I'm very well, thank you.
And you?'

'Oh—great. Just great,' responded Matthew flatly,
taking the trolley from her unresisting fingers. 'My car's
parked outside. It's in a restricted zone, so do you mind
if we move it?'

Olivia swallowed again, and, unable to prevent herself,
she put out a nervous hand and touched his sleeve. Beneath the fine leather of his jerkin his arm felt reassur-
ingly hard and muscular, and she felt his instinctive
rejection of her touch in the same instant that she pulled
her hand away.

'Sorry,' she murmured, making an issue of putting
the strap of her handbag over her shoulder, and Matthew
gave her a brief hard look.

'Is something wrong?' he enquired, and just for a
second she heard the edge of some stronger emotion in
his tone.

'No. No, nothing,' she answered, quickening her pace
deliberately. But she wondered what he would say if she
told him she had had to assure herself that he was real.

Years ago, Matthew had driven an old beaten-up Mini
that he and Sam Pollack, from Pollack's garage, had
worked on together until the engine sang as sweet as a
bird. It had been fast, too. Too fast, Olivia's father had
maintained, although in those days he had been more
concerned that Matthew's intentions were honourable.
After all, he was Lady Lavinia Ryan's son; and even if
his father was not *Sir* Matthew Ryan he did own Rycroft,
which in Lower Mychett was as good as owning a title.

The car that was parked outside was a far cry from
that old Mini however. It wasn't particularly clean, and
it was an estate, not a sports car. But it was a Mercedes;
Olivia recognised that at once. And, judging by the size
of its engine, it would be able to hold its own in any
contest.

Matthew swung open the passenger door, and nodded
at Olivia. 'You get in,' he said. 'I'll handle the luggage.'

Olivia caught her lower lip between her teeth. 'Oh—thanks,' she said, twisting the strap of her bag round her hand, as she eased herself into the wide, comfortable seat. But, now it seemed virtually certain that this was not some strange fantasy, other thoughts were asserting themselves. Not least, what was Matthew doing here? And who had asked him to come?

The car rocked as he slammed the tail-gate and, pushing the trolley aside, he came round the car and got in beside her. Folding his long legs beneath the wheel, he reached for his seatbelt, and Olivia permitted herself a fleeting look at his unyielding profile.

He hadn't changed much at all, she thought reluctantly, aware of his muscled thigh only inches away from her own. He had always been reasonably tall—around six feet, she guessed—which had made her five feet eight inches so much less of a problem. Until she had started going out with Matthew, she had usually been as tall as, or taller than, the boys she had dated. Matthew was a little heavier, she decided, but that was to be expected. He was older. Thirty-two now, to her twenty-eight. How well she knew that equation.

His face had aged more than his body, she noticed. There were lines beside his nose and mouth, and his grey eyes were set more deeply. But his hair was just as dark, and as usual needed cutting, catching his collar at the back, and tempting her to put it straight.

But it was then, as she dipped her head to avoid his cool appraisal, that she noticed the ring on his left hand. Her stomach hollowed at the realisation that it was a wedding-ring, and, although she knew she had no right to feel the way she did at that moment, a feeling of absolute nausea swept over her.

She thought she was going to be sick. For one awful moment, she really thought she might throw up, there, in Matthew's car, the feeling was so intense. But, somehow, she fought it back, though her forehead beaded with perspiration in the process. Dear God, she thought, surreptitiously wiping the back of her hand

across her temples, it shouldn't matter to her what
Matthew had done in the years since their separation.
It was perfectly reasonable that he should have found
someone else, that he should get married, and probably
start a family. That was what most men did, after all,
and a man as attractive to the opposite sex as Matthew
had always been was unlikely to have stayed single for
too long.

Nevertheless, as the feeling of sickness subsided, Olivia
knew that she was still not entirely objective where
Matthew was concerned. Briefly, she had known again
all the pain of that earlier betrayal, and, while it was
easy to dismiss their relationship from a distance, a one-
to-one confrontation was something else entirely.

In spite of her efforts to avoid his attention, the un-
evenness of her breathing could not be disguised, and
Matthew had always been fairly perceptive where she
was concerned.

'Are you ill?' he demanded, his attention torn between concern—and curiosity—about her welfare, and
the heavy pressure of traffic around the airport. 'For
God's sake, why didn't you tell me you weren't feeling
well before you got into the car?'

'I—just felt—sick, for a moment,' Olivia protested,
wondering what he would say if she told him the truth.
But then, he would probably enjoy the vindication of
believing she had regretted severing their relationship.
Whatever, the truth was not hers to tell, and that was
all there was to it.

'Hmm.' Matthew sounded impatient, and she wondered if he believed her. Still, he opened the electrically
controlled windows, and the cool draught of air was
marvellously refreshing. 'We'll find a service area, and
pull off and have some coffee,' he said, giving her
another glancing look. 'Didn't you have breakfast on
the plane?'

'I wasn't hungry,' admitted Olivia, smoothing her
damp palms over her knees. 'Airline food is so tasteless.'
She licked her dry lips. 'Don't you think?'

'I probably haven't travelled as much as you,' responded Matthew, keeping his eyes on the road. Then, braking to avoid a reckless queue-jumping motorcyclist, he added flatly, 'You don't look as though you eat enough these days.'

'Oh, thanks.' Olivia's response was tight and defensive. 'I really appreciate hearing that you think I look under-nourished!'

'I didn't say that.

Matthew's response was clipped, but Olivia was in no mood to consider the incongruity of this conversation. 'Didn't you?' she retorted. 'Well, it may interest you to know that where I come from you can't be *too* thin!'

'Or too rich, so I hear,' responded Matthew caustically. 'I suppose you can't have one without the other, can you?'

Olivia took a deep breath. 'Is that supposed to mean something?'

Matthew shrugged. Then, 'No,' he said, shaking his head, as if thinking better of arguing with her. 'I was just making polite conversation, that's all.' He deftly moved the Mercedes into the lane that would take them on to the M3 motorway, and merged with the traffic coming from the east. 'There's—er—there's a service area around here somewhere. Yes, there's the sign. It's just a couple of miles further on.'

'You don't have to stop for me,' said Olivia shortly, aware of a feeling of tension out of all proportion to what he had been saying, but Matthew just gave her a speaking look.

'We're stopping,' he said, putting his words into action as the slip-road for the service area came in sight. 'I could do with some coffee myself. It was barely half-past-six when I left home this morning.'

Olivia's lips tightened. 'Why did you come, anyway?' she asked ungraciously. 'I could have managed.'

'Could you?' Matthew swung the big car into a parking bay, and switched off the engine. 'Well, your mother asked me if I would, and how could I refuse?

She and your father, and the rest of the family, are pretty cut up about the old lady's death, you know. It's been fairly rough for them, ever since she had that first stroke, just before Christmas.'

Olivia stared at him. 'She had a stroke before Christmas?' she exclaimed. She shook her head. 'I didn't know.'

'No. Well, I guess they didn't think you'd be interested,' said Matthew evenly, thrusting open the door. He paused. 'Are you coming? Or are you determined to make this even more difficult than it already is?'

Olivia caught her breath, as she scrambled out. 'More difficult?' she echoed, aware that he could misinterpret the indignation in her tone. But it wasn't fair that he should make judgements about her. She hadn't known about her grandmother's illness, and he had no idea how painful this all was.

'Yes, more difficult,' Matthew said now, slamming the car door and locking it. 'Don't remind me what a selfish little bitch you are!'

Olivia stared at him through tear-glazed eyes. 'I didn't ask you to come,' she exclaimed, taking refuge in the childish retort, and Matthew sighed.

'No,' he conceded, after a moment. 'You didn't ask me to come. And you're making it bloody plain you wish I hadn't.' He glanced round, as if assuring himself that their conversation was not being overheard, and then added wearily, 'But, please—don't make a scene here! For your grandmother's sake, I'm prepared to forget the past, and so should you. Ten years is too long for me to bear a grudge—or for you to feel a sense of guilt!'

CHAPTER TWO

THE sun came out as they sat at a table by the window, in the self-service restaurant. It streamed through the faintly dusty panes, bathing Olivia in its light, and soothing her raw emotions. She had made no response to Matthew's final accusation in the car park, and now she sat staring at the coffee in her cup, wondering again why she had been so foolish as to respond to her mother's telegram. After all, no one had asked her to come and, whatever Matthew said, ten years was not long enough to heal some wounds.

Not that he seemed to be suffering too badly, she thought uncharitably, her eyes straying to the brown, long-fingered hands gripping the knife and fork across the table from her. Matthew was tucking into bacon, eggs and fried tomatoes with apparent relish, and Olivia envied him his ability to ignore her evidently unwelcome presence.

He had nice hands, she reflected unwillingly, a tremor of awareness causing an unwanted shiver to slide down her spine. Once, those hands had been as familiar to her as her own, and when they were together they had seldom been far from hers. If they weren't holding hands, he had had his arm about her shoulders, and she had revelled in the possessive pressure he had displayed. She had wanted him to touch her; she had wanted to touch him just as urgently, and when they were alone——

She caught herself up short, swallowing a hasty mouthful of her coffee and almost scalding her mouth in the process. But allowing her thoughts to drift in that direction was not only wrong, but futile, and she made a determined effort to rekindle the sense of resentment his cool, disparaging comments had aroused in her. Only so long as she could maintain some feeling of anger towards him could she hope to sustain her detachment. She had not realised how fatally easy it would be to delude herself about their relationship, or that, even knowing who he was, she might still *want* him. Time had changed a lot of things, it was true, and the idealistic young girl she had been when she'd boarded the plane for the United States was gone forever. But because she was older, and more experienced in the ways of the world, she was also more tolerant of human frailty. Not least her own. She was realising that those years had also blunted the edge of her conviction.

Dangerously so, she acknowledged now, giving Matthew another covert glance. She would never have believed she could still be attracted to him. But he had been her first love, after all, and didn't they say that you never forgot your first love?

He lifted his eyes from his plate then, and caught her looking at him. And she had to steel herself to meet the cool challenge in his gaze. She wondered if he suspected what she was thinking. Once, he had been able to interpret her every expression, but that was before she had learned the art of dissimulation. Nevertheless, his gaze was disturbingly intent, and it took all her powers of resistance to withstand the desire to look away.

'Don't,' he said after a moment, putting down his knife and fork and wiping his mouth with the back of his hand. Then, picking up the cup beside his plate, he emptied its contents and set it down. 'Drink your coffee, Olivia. It's time to go.'

'Is it?' Perversely, Olivia was disposed to linger. It was crazy, she knew, but there was one sure way of retaining the animosity between them, and that was by provoking his anger, too. 'I was just thinking I might have some breakfast, after all.' She gave the buffet shelves a provocative appraisal. 'A hot Danish, perhaps. That's what I usually have at home.'

Matthew's mouth tightened. 'Very well,' he said. 'I'll wait for you in the car. Don't hurry. I'll buy a paper, and catch up on the morning news.'

Olivia stared at him. 'You'd do that, wouldn't you?' she exclaimed indignantly. 'After I've sat and watched you wolf down the most revolting mess of fried food I've ever seen!'

Matthew's lips twitched. 'You're talking about the great British breakfast,' he told her sardonically. 'We're not all health freaks.'

Olivia wanted to tell him that the amount of cholesterol he had swallowed that morning would go a fair way to clogging his arteries, but she refused to let him gain the upper hand. And besides, it had to be said, he didn't look as if he suffered any ill effects. On the contrary, he looked disgustingly healthy, and observing his tanned skin she wondered exactly what kind of occupation he had chosen.

'Well, anyway,' she said, back-tracking, 'we're not in any great hurry, are we?'

'You may not be,' remarked Matthew, but he remained in his seat, and Olivia moistened her dry lips.

'Does that mean you are?'

'I do have responsibilities,' conceded Matthew evenly. 'Oh, go on. Get yourself a Danish, if that's what you want. I must admit, if you were feeling sick earlier, food is probably what you need.'

Olivia looked across at him. 'Will you get it for me? I—er—I don't have any change.'

Matthew gave her an old-fashioned look, but he got to his feet and walked back to the buffet, flexing his shoulders as he did so. He was wearing jeans with his jerkin, and a pair of worn leather boots, like the ones he used to wear when they were together. She watched him as he exchanged a smiling comment with the girl on the pay-till, and she felt a stabbing sense of envy. He should be smiling at her, not at some stranger, she thought painfully. He had such a nice smile, and when he was relaxed the years just fell away.

'There you are,' he said, setting the plate containing the apricot Danish pastry down in front of her. 'Hot, as you ordered, but probably nowhere near as delicious as *you're* used to.'

Olivia looked up at him, as he made no move to drop into the seat opposite. 'Don't be like that,' she said, unconsciously using all her charm to persuade him to stay. 'You're not really going, are you?'

Matthew's eyes darkened perceptibly. 'Liv——'

'That's the first time you've called me that!' she exclaimed, digging her fork into the Danish, and lifting a sugary morsel to her lips. Her tongue came out to accept the delicate mouthful, and in Matthew's eyes she saw a reflection of the torment she was feeling.

'I'm married, Olivia,' he said in a strangled voice, and although the news was no real surprise to her it still had the power to constrict her throat.

'So—what?' she managed, swallowing the fragment of pastry with a valiant effort. 'I only want to talk to you.'

Matthew hesitated, but after a moment he subsided into his seat again, and only the heaviness with which he did so revealed his reluctance to accede to her request. 'All right,' he said. 'Talk. I'm listening.'

Olivia dragged her eyes away from his, and made an issue of detaching a slice of apricot from its sticky base. 'It's not that easy,' she said, knowing she should have let him go. Playing games with Matthew Ryan was quite simply playing with fire. She knew the dangers. She knew the risks. And yet, she couldn't seem to help herself.

'I guess—I guess I just want us to be friends,' she said, at last, lifting her eyes from her plate. 'As you said, ten years is an awfully long time.'

'No way!' Matthew lay back in his chair, and regarded her with barely disguised hostility. 'I said I was prepared to forget the past, and I am. But that doesn't mean I want us to be friends.'

'But isn't that a contradiction in terms?' Olivia sighed. 'How can you say you're prepared to forget something, and then use that something as a reason for rejecting any contact between us?'

'I'm not interested in discussing it.' Matthew ran an impatient hand through his hair. 'Now, do you mind getting on with that, if you really want it?'

'But—we're different people,' protested Olivia, putting down her fork and unconsciously leaning towards him. 'You're—married, as you say. And I'm—involved—with somebody. We don't know anything about one another really. And—and I'd like to know about you. I would. Purely objectively, of course. Wouldn't that be more—civilised?'

'*Civilised!*' Matthew almost choked on the word, and a wave of colour invaded his face. 'What was ever civilised about our relationship? You don't know the meaning of the word. You *used* me, Olivia. You let me think you cared about me as much as I cared about you. But you didn't. It was all a game to you. You just wanted the experience of knowing how crazy I was about you! Well, not any more. I learned my lesson well. You won't ever make a fool of me again.'

Olivia gasped. 'I didn't make a fool of you——'

'Didn't you?' Matthew's expression was bitter, and he came forward in his chair, so that he could thrust his face close to hers. 'And I suppose having the girl you had told everyone you were going to marry clear off to the States with a guitar player wasn't a humiliating experience?'

'It wasn't like that.' Olivia shook her head. 'You know I went as the Kramers' nanny. Stephen Kramer wasn't interested in me. He was far too much in love with Denise.'

'All I know is, one minute we were talking about setting up house together, and the next you're jumping on a plane to New York. It was pretty mortifying, I can tell you. Not to mention emotionally shattering. My God, you seduced me, Olivia! And you sit there and talk about civility!'

Olivia swallowed. *'I—seduced you!'* She caught her
breath. 'Have you forgotten, I hadn't even been to bed
with a man, until you—until you made love to me?'

'I didn't make love *to* you, I made love *with* you,'
Matthew corrected her, in a low impassioned tone. 'Oh,
what's the use? Love's another word that doesn't figure
very highly in your vocabulary, isn't it? Come on. Let's
go. I don't propose to discuss this any longer.'

Pressing his palms down on the table, he got to his
feet, and towered over her. 'Are you coming?' he demanded grimly, and Olivia bent her head. She didn't
have a lot of choice, and he knew it.

But, as she followed his stalking path to the door, resentment flared anew. Some of what he had said she
could not dispute. But she refused to accept that she had
been wholly responsible for the development of their relationship. Dear God, she had been a total innocent when
she'd first gone to his rooms at the university. He
couldn't blame her for seducing him. Not when he had
taught her all she knew about...

Her anger was instinctive, and uncontrollable. For a
few brief moments indignation blinded her, and as they
walked through the swing glass doors she caught his arm.

'I don't care what you say—you *wanted* me!' she declared huskily, gazing up into his narrowed eyes, and
with a muffled oath Matthew put out his hand and
grasped her nape with strong, unyielding fingers.

'I know that, dammit,' he swore, the pressure of his
fingers increasing. And then, before she truly realised
what he intended to do, he bent his head and brought
her lips to his.

Olivia's senses swam. She couldn't help it. It had happened so quickly, so unexpectedly, and the sudden heat
of his mouth against her parted lips made her dizzy. In
consequence, instead of pushing him away, she clutched
the front of his shirt, and a button parted to allow her
fingers to brush the hair-roughened skin beneath.

'Christ!'

The revulsion of Matthew's withdrawal was like a slap in the face, and Olivia opened her eyes to find him striding away in obvious agitation. But it was nothing compared to the agitation she was feeling, and the horror that enveloped her at the thought that, whatever she had expected, nothing had changed. Matthew was still the only man who could turn her bones to water, and that realisation was enough to make her wish she had never left New York.

A man, who looked as if he might be a sales representative, emerged from the building behind her, and paused to give her a concerned look. 'You feeling OK?' he asked, his eyes moving approvingly over her slim, attractive figure, and Olivia summoned up the energy to give him a tight smile.

'Um—yes, thank you,' she replied, after a moment. 'Just—taking a breather, that's all.'

'Ah.' The man nodded, and then, glancing over his shoulder, he added, 'Looks as if he's getting impatient, hmm?'

'Who—*oh*!' Olivia gasped in dismay, as she saw the Mercedes heading towards the exit. It was moving slowly, but there was no mistaking its intention, and, gesturing helplessly at the man beside her, she started after it.

A few yards from the restaurant, she broke into a run, catching up with estate car fairly easily, but not without soaking herself in perspiration. 'You—you bastard!' she exclaimed, jerking open the door and scrambling inside, and Matthew gave her a dark, hooded, look.

'I can't help it if you choose to make eyes at every man you see,' he retorted coldly, accelerating into the filter lane, and Olivia caught her breath at the cutting accusation.

'I was not making eyes at anyone,' she exclaimed, struggling to fasten her seatbelt, and Matthew's mouth twisted.

'He didn't get past you, though, did he?' he taunted. 'What did you say to him? Did you tell him I was mistreating you?'

'No!' Olivia glared at him. 'As a matter of fact, *he* spoke to *me*! He asked if I was all right, that's all.'

'Really?'

'Yes, really.' Olivia found her own anger was dissipating in the face of Matthew's obvious resentment. 'What's the matter?' she demanded recklessly. 'Are you jealous?'

He didn't answer her. But then, she hadn't really expected him to. So much for her hopes that she and Matthew might be able to salvage something from the wreck of their relationship, she thought wearily. All they seemed capable of doing was hurting one another. Well, he could hurt her, she appended. More than he knew, or would ever know.

Expelling a breath of air in an upward draught over her hot face, she unbuttoned the neck of her shirt. It seemed unseasonably hot for England, but then, she had just sprinted a hundred yards. It was lucky she was wearing low-heeled shoes. In high heels she'd never have made it.

Or would she? Would Matthew really have driven away and left her? Somehow, she doubted it. But perhaps she was being unduly optimistic. It was obvious he despised her—and what her incautious accusation had made him do.

Realising there was still at least another hour to go to their destination, Olivia decided to try again. After all, they could hardly arrive at her parents' house not speaking to one another. Surely there was some way she could appeal to his common sense.

Moistening her lips, she said softly, 'So—tell me about your wife. How long have you been married?' And, the hardest question of all, 'Do you have any children?'

She thought he wasn't going to answer her. The silence between them stretched oppressively, and the heat of Olivia's body wouldn't subside. She told herself it was because the sun was shining, and the car was getting warm, but that wasn't the reason. The truth was, her high temperature was self-induced, brought on by her awareness of the man behind the wheel.

And then, as she was casting about in her mind for something else to say, he said abruptly, 'You were right, of course. I was jealous.'

It was the last thing she had expected him to say, and Olivia found it difficult to get her breath. 'Matt——'

'Oh, don't worry,' he interrupted her swiftly, his tone self-denigrating. 'I don't intend to do anything about it. It's just an aberration, and I'll get over it. I did it before, and I can do it again. I just have to keep reminding myself what a little tramp you are.'

Olivia swallowed the instinctive desire to defend herself. It was probably safer to let Matthew believe what he liked about her. Being friendly with him wasn't going to work. Not for him; not for her; probably not for anybody.

Pressing her trembling lips together, she held up her head. 'So,' she said, adopting a deliberately mild tone, 'why don't you tell me about your wife? Who is she? Do I know her?'

Matthew gave her a contemptuous look. 'Why should I talk to you about my wife?' he demanded. 'You don't have to humour me, Olivia. I won't embarrass you in front of your parents, if that's what you're afraid of.'

Olivia sighed. 'I'm not afraid of anything,' she retorted heavily. 'For heaven's sake, Matt, I'm just trying to find some common ground between us. Something we can talk about, without ending up at one another's throats——'

'And do you imagine talking about my marriage will accomplish that?' Matthew demanded scathingly. 'I hardly think so. Still, Helen is nothing like you, I can tell you that.'

'Helen?' Olivia frowned. 'Not—Helen Berrenger?'

'No. Helen *Ryan*,' said Matthew succinctly. 'We've been married nearly ten years.'

'You mean...'

But Olivia found she couldn't go on. It was too painful. To think that he must have married Helen only months after they split up! It hurt. Helen Berrenger, she thought disbelievingly. Helen, who had always been more interested in horses than anything else. But eminently suitable, she couldn't deny that. Her lineage went back almost as far as Matthew's, and her father, Conrad Berrenger, owned a string of racehorses, as well as a generous portion of the county.

Her silence was noticeable, and eventually Matthew cast a glance in her direction. 'Well?' he demanded harshly. 'What did you expect? An undying commitment?'

'*No!*' Olivia was defensive. 'Of course not. But—Helen Berrenger!'

'Why not?' Matthew's dark brows ascended. 'I wasn't about to make another mistake.'

'What do you mean?'

'I mean, Helen would never have done what you did,' he retorted coldly. 'She understands about things like—honour—and integrity.'

'And I don't, is that it?' Olivia flared, using some of the hurt she was feeling to fuel her defence. 'Oh, don't tell me—it's the old class system, isn't it? My father is only one of your father's tenants, so naturally I don't have the right pedigree——'

'Don't you dare say that,' Matthew overrode her angrily. 'And don't think you can assuage your own guilt by turning it on me. You know damn well there was never any question of your not being good enough for my family. Both my parents liked you, you know that. You were always made to feel at home at Rycroft. Hell, they were as shocked as I was when you walked out!'

'Even so——'

'Even so nothing. Any contempt they feel for you now is entirely justified. My God, my father actually wanted me to go after you. He offered to pay my fare, so I could try and persuade you to come back.'

Olivia swallowed. 'But you didn't.'

'No, I didn't.' Matthew's lips twisted. 'I still had some pride. And besides, your grandmother told me your leaving wasn't a spur-of-the-moment thing. Apparently, you'd been planning it for some time.'

'That's not—*oh*!'

Olivia pressed a hand to her mouth to prevent herself from voicing the instinctive denial. What good would it do now to try and explain herself? How could she explain herself, without betraying the very people she had gone away to protect? It was ironic, really, that Matthew's father should have wanted him to go after her. But then, he was as ignorant of his responsibilities as Matthew himself.

'That's not what?' Matthew asked now, as the traffic thinned, and he was able to give her more of his attention. 'The way it was? Well? How was it? You tell me. Tell me how you came to get that job with the Kramers, if you didn't answer an advertisement?' He grimaced. 'An advertisement I knew nothing about.'

Olivia sighed. What was the point? she thought tiredly. She could have explained that her brother, Andrew, had met Stephen Kramer, when they were at school, and that, although Stephen was older, when his family had moved away to London the two of them had kept in touch, but she didn't. It was probably better if Matthew continued to believe what her grandmother had told him. Although she might feel better if he stopped hating her, what would that really achieve?

'All right,' she said, twisting to stare out of the window. 'I behaved badly. I admit it. But——' her skin prickled '—as you and Helen got together so—quickly, I probably did you a favour.' She turned her head. 'Didn't I?'

A pulse in Matthew's jaw was beating rapidly, but he didn't say anything. He just gave her a contemptuous look, and Olivia had to be content with knowing she had averted any chance of a reconciliation.

They left the M3 at Winchester, and after circling the old Roman town took the road to Abbot's Norton. They

didn't stop again, even though Olivia would have welcomed another drink, and by half-past eleven they were
cresting the hill that ran down into Lower Mychett.

It was all achingly familiar now, and Olivia had to
press the palms of her hands together to prevent herself
from revealing how nervous she was. She had to force
herself to sit still, too. The need to pluck the legs of her
trousers away from her damp body was almost
overwhelming.

Lower Mychett lay in some of the most beautiful
countryside in England, and as Matthew drove down
the winding road to the village Olivia had plenty of time
to absorb the view. The grey spire of the church was still
the most obvious landmark, with the River Mychett em-
bracing the churchyard, before flowing under Fox
Bridge. The river divided Lower Mychett from its
neighbour, Upper Mychett, and the Rycroft estate owned
most of both.

Fortunately, as it was almost lunchtime, there were
not a lot of people about, although there were children
playing outside the post office cum general stores, and
several old people were seated on the bench beside the
green. Of course, they all recognised Matthew's car,
thought Olivia bitterly, as he raised his hand again, in
acknowledgement of someone's greeting. Everyone knew
and respected the Ryans. And not just because they controlled the village's livelihood.

'Isn't that Jenny Mason?' exclaimed Olivia, suddenly,
stung out of her reticence by the sight of a girl she had
once gone to school with, wheeling a twin pushchair
containing two toddlers across the street. A third child,
of perhaps four or five, trailed along behind, and Olivia
stared at her disbelievingly, hardly recognising her friend.

'That's right,' said Matthew flatly, apparently realising that they were nearing their destination, and that
he would have to appear to be sociable for her parents'
sake. 'Except that she's Jenny Innes now. She married
your brother's friend, Tony.'

Olivia shook her head. 'Jenny married Tony Innes,' she echoed blankly. 'But she was the cleverest girl in the class. I thought she was going to university. She always wanted to be a teacher.'

'Well, we don't always get what we want, do we?' observed Matthew, his hands flexing on the steering-wheel. 'She obviously thought more about Innes than getting a degree.' He shrugged. 'Some people do the craziest things when they're in love.'

Olivia sighed. 'Nevertheless,' she said patiently, 'you know what Tony Innes was like. And, looking at Jenny, it doesn't appear that he's changed.'

'So what?' Matthew's mouth compressed. 'Why should it matter to you?'

'Because Jenny was my friend,' retorted Olivia shortly. And now she looks tired, and disillusioned, she added silently, watching the way the other woman turned and, catching the hand of the little boy, who was walking behind her, yanked him up to the pushchair. Jenny looked worn, and tight-lipped, and if she hadn't known better Olivia would have taken her for a woman of nearly forty.

'You didn't keep in touch with her while you've been away, I gather,' Matthew commented drily, and Olivia hunched her shoulders.

'No.'

'Not such a good friend, then,' he remarked, as she turned to look back over her shoulder. 'I doubt if Jenny wants your sympathy. She's probably forgotten you ever existed.'

Olivia pressed her lips together for a moment. Then, 'That's a rotten thing to say,' she said at last, as Matthew turned on to the road that led to the Stoners' farm. 'We weren't that close. Not really. I mean, by the time I was seventeen——'

She broke off then, realising what she had been about to say, but Matthew chose to finish the sentence for her.

'By the time you were seventeen, *we* didn't have time for anyone else,' he said grimly. 'Did we? I came home every weekend, so that we could be together.'

'I know.'

Olivia's response was barely audible, and Matthew uttered a harsh expletive. 'I could have killed you, you know,' he muttered, in a bitter voice. 'I wanted to. I think that's why I didn't go after you. I didn't trust myself. And your family had suffered enough.'

Olivia shivered, but then, seeing the look in his eyes, she frowned. 'My family?'

'Well—your mother,' he said, obviously expecting her to understand. 'It wouldn't have been fair to cause her any more—— '

'My mother?' broke in Olivia blankly. 'What are you talking about? Why should you single out my mother? Oh—you mean because of her angina——'

'No. Not her angina,' said Matthew shortly. He glanced her way, and then gave her a more studied look. 'But—you must know.'

Olivia was getting anxious. 'Must know what?'

'That—that your mother had a heart attack, the day after you left home? Do you mean to say you don't know she's been confined to a wheelchair ever since?'

CHAPTER THREE

OLIVIA couldn't sleep. For over an hour she tossed and turned in the unfamiliar bed, and then, unable to stand the torment of her thoughts any longer, she threw back the sheet.

The silk wrap, which matched the oyster satin nightgown she was wearing, was lying at the foot of the bed, and she put it on. Perhaps if she went downstairs and made herself a warm drink it would help her to relax, she thought. Whatever, she had to escape from the bedroom, and the steady sound of Sara snoring in the other bed.

Evidently her sister harboured no uneasy memories, Olivia reflected wryly, as moonlight illuminated Sara's sleeping form. But then, her sister was heavily pregnant with her first child, and probably needed her sleep more than most. Like Olivia, she had arrived today, but only from Portsmouth. Married to a naval rating, Sara lived in married quarters there, and she had come home for her grandmother's funeral.

Opening the door as quietly as she could, Olivia slipped out on to the landing of the old farmhouse. Although the landing was carpeted, the boards squeaked beneath her feet, and she stifled a sigh. She had never been able to sneak downstairs without announcing her coming. It had been quite a feat, when she and Sara were younger, to raid the larder without their parents knowing. But it was years since she had trod these stairs, and she had forgotten which of them to avoid.

Still, she made it to the kitchen without any apparent disturbance and, switching on the light, she went to fill the kettle. An old cat, which might or might not have been the tabby they had had when she went away, miaowed appealingly as she took the milk from the fridge, and, although she was sure it must have had its ration for the day, she filled its dish with some of the creamy liquid. She had forgotten what real milk tasted like, she reflected, licking a drop from her finger. She had become so used to the skimmed variety.

She was pouring a mug of tea when the kitchen door opened, and her hand shook a little as her father came into the room. In his dressing-gown and slippers, he seemed slightly less remote than he had appeared earlier in the day, though his features were unforgiving as they viewed his older daughter.

'I hope you don't mind.' Olivia stumbled into words, feeling distinctly like an interloper. 'I couldn't sleep, so I thought I'd make myself a drink. Would—would you like some?'

'Not for me.' Robert Stoner approached the table, and she thought how much older he looked now than when she had left. His hair was almost completely grey, and his lean frame was prematurely stooped. 'Your mother heard you come downstairs,' he added, looking down at the teapot with unseeing eyes. 'She sent me to investigate.'

'Oh, I see.' Olivia moistened her lips with her tongue. 'Um—well, do you think she would like——?'

'Your mother doesn't drink tea at night,' declared her father heavily. 'It makes her restless.'

'Oh.' Olivia bit down on the inside of her lower lip. 'I'm sorry—sorry if I disturbed you, that is. I—I never thought.'

'No.'

There was a wealth of meaning in that one word, and Olivia sank down on to one of the wooden kitchen chairs. So much for hoping her father might have forgiven her, she thought wearily. If she had known yesterday what she knew now, would she still have made the trip from New York?

'I'll leave you to drink your tea, then.'

Robert Stoner moved back towards the door, and, risking another rebuff, Olivia got to her feet. 'Please,' she said. 'Won't you at least stay while I drink my tea? We—we haven't exchanged more than a dozen words since I got here. Don't you think we could try to make amends? For—for Mum's sake, at least.'

Her father turned. 'For your mother's sake!' he exclaimed angrily. 'Since when have you ever cared about your mother?'

'I've always cared about my mother—and you,' replied Olivia huskily. 'For heaven's sake, Dad, what did I do that was so terrible? Nothing more than what thousands of other girls do every day!'

'You can stand there and say that, when you know what it did to your mother?' said her father harshly, and Olivia sighed.

'I didn't know what—what happened to Mum,' she protested.

'But you never bothered to come home to find out, did you?'

'Oh, Dad, I wanted you to come to New York. When—when you didn't——'

'You forgot about us, right?'

'Wrong.' Olivia pushed back the weight of her hair with a trembling hand. 'I thought—oh, I don't know what I thought. That you hadn't forgiven me, I suppose.' She looked at him helplessly. 'And you haven't.'

'What did you expect?' Robert Stoner's face was bitter. 'It hasn't been easy for us, Livvy. We could have done with another pair of hands around the house, particularly since your grandmother was taken ill. But you didn't care, did you? You were too busy making a lot of money; getting yourself involved with God knows how many other men! Shaming your mother and me by pretending young Matt wasn't good enough for you.'

Olivia's cheeks flamed with colour. 'It wasn't like that——'

'Wasn't it?' Her father came back to rest his hands on the table. 'Let me tell you, that's exactly what it was like. Do you have any idea what could have happened to us when you turned Matt down?'

Olivia swallowed. 'What do you mean?'

'I mean, we're tenants here, Livvy. This house, the land it stands on, the land that gives us our livelihood, is *Ryan* property. How would it have been if old Matthew Ryan had decided to throw us out——'

'He wouldn't!'

'He could have.' Her father's knuckles were white against the weathered skin of his hands. 'He had that right, Livvy. And when you threw young Matt over, there was some in the village who thought it was nought but what we deserved.'

Olivia shook her head. 'He wouldn't have done it,' she said again, but there was less conviction in her voice now. What had Matthew said? That he had wanted to kill her? If his father had felt even half the anger his son had felt at what she had done revenge might have sounded very sweet.

'Anyway, he didn't,' she tendered, in a small voice, and her father's lips curled.

'No. Because your mother was rushed to hospital, the day after you went away, and the Ryans had compassion for our situation. Young Matt even came and helped Andy, while I spent time at the hospital. My God, I hope you found what you were looking for, because I doubt you'll ever meet a finer man than Matt Ryan!'

'Bob! Your voice carries all over the house!'

The door behind him had opened, and now Felicity Stoner wheeled herself into the room. Since her mother's heart attack, one of the downstairs rooms had been converted into the bedroom, which her parents occupied. Now, Mrs Stoner looked questioningly from her husband to her daughter and back again, and then shook her head reprovingly as she comprehended what was going on.

'Cissie, what are you doing out of bed?'

Robert Stoner's voice altered amazingly when he spoke to his wife, but for once she did not respond to its warm solicitude. 'Never mind what I'm doing, what are you doing?' she exclaimed impatiently. 'For heaven's sake, Bob, the girl's barely been in the house five minutes, and already you're encouraging her to leave again.'

'I am not!'

Her husband was indignant, but Olivia's mother was equally adamant. 'Yes, you are,' she said. 'I heard at least a part of what you were saying, and I want you to know I don't agree with you. What was the point of Olivia's marrying Matt if she wasn't in love with him? Would you have had them live a miserable life together, just because you were afraid of offending the Ryans?'

It was fair, and it was reasonable, and Olivia just wished she had thought of that explanation. But then, she hadn't left because she wasn't in love with Matt; rather because she was.

But, not for the first time, she looked at her mother with wondering eyes. Felicity Stoner seemed so frail and defenceless, and yet, at times, she could assert a remarkable strength of purpose. For instance, never once, in any of the letters she had exchanged with her daughter, had she so much as hinted at the deterioration of her condition. And here she was now, finding a perfectly reasonable explanation for Olivia's leaving home.

But Olivia didn't think it was pride, or a misplaced sense of compassion, that caused her mother to defend her. Even though she had never mentioned it to her daughter, she must have known why Olivia had chosen to leave. In spite of her grandmother's admonition to Olivia to keep what she had learned to herself, there had always been one other person who knew the truth. And that was her mother. Olivia wondered how far *she* would have let her relationship with Matthew go, before she had had to tell her daughter the truth.

Now, however, it was her father who was forced to defend himself. 'Things had to be said,' he muttered, giving his thinning hair a smoothing touch. 'Livvy can't come back here and think we're going to treat her like the prodigal daughter——'

'I don't think she expects that,' said Mrs Stoner drily. She gave her daughter a thoughtful look, and then her pale face broke into a smile. 'But *I* am glad to see her, whatever you say. And I'm hoping she won't run away again, as soon as your mother's funeral's over.'

Olivia's throat was suddenly tight with emotion, and, leaving the table, she approached her mother's chair. Kneeling down beside her, she felt the years just slip away, and when Felicity put a hand to her cheek she covered it with her own.

'I'd—I'd like to stay—for a little while,' she said, as her mother's thumb wiped an errant tear from her chin. Perry wasn't going to be too pleased, but Agnes could manage without her. 'I'm sorry about—about Grandmother, but I'm glad it gave me a reason to come.'

'You didn't need one,' declared her father roughly, but she saw his face had lost much of its cold severity. 'Now, I suggest we all try and get some sleep. The cows won't thank me if I'm late for early morning milking.'

The sun was streaming through the kitchen windows when Olivia came downstairs next morning. She had overslept—it was already after ten o'clock—but she felt so much more optimistic today.

The previous day now seemed like a bad dream. Her encounter with Matthew, her tense arrival at the house, and her subsequent confrontation with her father, had all combined to make her wish she hadn't come. But her mother had changed all that. With a few words she had cleared the air between them, and, although Olivia didn't delude herself that Robert Stoner was completely won over, at least they might be civil with one another.

The day before, the house had been full of friends and neighbours, all of whom had come to offer their condolences. In one way, it had made it easier for Olivia; she had felt like just another visitor, and certainly her father had made her feel like an outsider. But in another it had made it harder; she had known that sooner or later she would be called to account, and even her sister, Sara, had treated her like a stranger.

Well, she supposed, they were strangers, after all. Sara had only been fourteen when Olivia went away. Now, she was twenty-four, a young married woman, on the verge of having her own family to care for. What did they know about one another really? Only what their mother had conveyed to them, through the medium of her letters.

However, it was her brother, Andrew, who was sitting at the kitchen table, sharing a pot of coffee with Enid Davis, the daily woman, when Olivia entered the room. Apparently Mrs Davis had been employed on a temporary basis, just after her grandmother had been taken ill. But, when it had become apparent that Harriet Stoner was not going to be able to do very much for herself, she had stayed on. Olivia had been introduced to her the day before, and although Mrs Davis was no one's idea of a rosy-cheeked retainer, she seemed competent enough.

Now, both she and Andrew rose as Olivia came into the room, and she shook her head disarmingly, urging them to stay where they were. 'Do carry on,' she said, conscious that her cream silk trousers and matching vest-top were coming under close scrutiny. 'I'll join you, if I may. It smells delicious.'

Her brother hesitated for a moment, and then subsided back into his seat, but Mrs Davis moved away from the table. 'I've finished,' she said, 'and I've got the bedrooms to see to. Oh,' she paused, 'unless you'd like me to get you some breakfast, Miss Stoner. We've home-cured bacon, and our own eggs, if you'd like some.'

Olivia shook her head, aware that if she had chosen to take the woman up on her offer it wouldn't have been welcomed. Tall and angular, Enid Davis had assumed an air of possessive authority, and even the way she said 'Miss Stoner' seemed to underline her opinion that Olivia was an outsider.

'I'll get myself some toast later, if I want it,' Olivia said now, collecting a cup from the pinewood dresser, and seating herself beside her brother. After all, she thought defensively, this was still her home. But she managed a tight smile anyway. 'Thank you.'

'If you say so, Miss Stoner.' Mrs Davis was evidently not prepared to make any concessions, and Olivia pulled a face as she marched out of the room.

'You really shouldn't make fun of Enid,' Andrew declared, as soon as the woman was out of earshot, and Olivia mentally drew a breath. 'She's been good to us, you know, and we all rely on her.'

'I wasn't making fun of her,' Olivia protested quietly. 'But—well, I do know where our bacon and eggs come from. And all this—*Miss* Stoner! Doesn't she know I used to live here?'

Andrew shrugged, and Olivia thought how much more like their father he had become. When she'd gone away, Andrew had been seventeen; still a boy really, and lots of fun to be with. After all, if it hadn't been for him, she might never have had the opportunity to go to the States. It was when he'd told her that the Kramers were thinking of getting a nanny, to look after their little girl while they were on tour, that the idea of applying for the job had occurred to her. And it had been due to Andrew's influence that she had got it. She had had little experience, when all was said and done, and none of it professional. But when she got to know him better Stephen had confessed that he had been dreading having to employ some snooty graduate from a nursing academy, and right from the beginning Olivia and Denise Kramer had really got along.

But now, Andrew was much more serious. He was married, too. She had met his wife the day before. But Laura, as she was called, had seemed shy and self-effacing, happiest with their two children, leaving Andrew to make the decisions.

'I expect she feels a bit uncomfortable with you,' Andrew volunteered now, and Olivia had to make an effort to remember what they had been talking about.

'Oh—Mrs Davis,' she said, pouring herself a cup of black coffee, and inhaling the aroma. 'I don't think it's that at all.' She smiled ruefully. 'Perhaps she's afraid her position is being threatened. The prodigal's return, and all that jazz.'

Andrew snorted. 'Don't be silly,' he said, pushing his own cup aside. 'Why should Enid feel threatened by you? You're hardly likely to want to get your hands dirty, are you? I mean——' he gave her a scathing appraisal '—that's hardly the outfit for swilling out the barn.'

'And is that what Mrs Davis does?' enquired Olivia coolly, realising Andrew was only reflecting his father's attitude, and her brother coloured.

'No——'

'So why should I be expected to do it?' Olivia regarded him steadily. 'I'm sorry if you don't like what I'm wearing, but it's cool and comfortable, and washes very easily.'

Andrew's jaw hardened. 'I didn't mean that, and you know it.'

'Do I?'

'Yes.' He blustered. 'I mean, this is just a duty visit for you. You'll go to Gran's funeral tomorrow, pay your last respects, and then you'll be off again. Back to New York, with your swish friends, and your swish flat——'

Olivia gasped. 'How do you know I live in a *swish* flat, as you call it? You've never even seen it.'

'No. But I've heard plenty about it,' he retorted. 'Mum reads us all your letters, you know. About what you've been doing, and where you've been——'

'Then you must also know that for the first five years I was in New York I lived in a one-bedroom walk-up in Queens,' declared Olivia hotly. 'Believe me, there's nothing swish about Queens. But I worked hard—and

I saved—and eventually, *eventually*, I managed to buy
the lease of a small apartment on the lower east side.'

Andrew's mouth curled. 'You *saved*!'

'Yes, I saved.'

'And what about Perry Randall? I suppose he didn't
make a contribution.'

Olivia sighed. 'Perry helped me, yes. But it was my
idea to start an agency for British nannies in New York,
and it was because of its success that I was able to afford
something better. Heavens, Stephen helped me as much
as anyone; surely you know that? Perry just thought I
was a good investment, that's all. It—it wasn't until later
that—that——'

'That you became his mistress,' finished Andrew disparagingly, and Olivia had to steel herself not to slap his
smug face.

'It wasn't easy, living alone,' she said instead. 'You've
always had a family to support you. I haven't.'

'And whose fault is that?' demanded Andrew harshly.
'I was a fool. I should never have let you persuade me
to ask Stephen to take you with him. I suppose I never
thought you'd really go. And then, when Mum had her
heart attack, Dad blamed me.'

'Did he?' Olivia expelled her breath unsteadily. That
explained a lot. She should have realised their father
would need to find a scapegoat. Much as she loved him,
she was not blind to his failings.

'Anyway, it's nothing to do with me what you do with
your life,' Andrew declared now. 'If you ask me, Matt
was well rid of you. I never thought a sister of mine
would get a reputation for sleeping around——'

'I do *not* sleep around,' protested Olivia. 'And if
you're talking about Perry again, I should tell you that
he *has* asked me to marry him.'

Andrew looked sulky. 'Are you going to?'

'I don't know.'

'You don't know?'

'No.' Olivia shook her head. 'Look, Andy, just because you still imagine that marriage is the be all and

end all of everything don't expect everyone to feel the same. I'm an independent woman; I have my own business. How I choose to spend the rest of my life, and with whom, is no one's concern but mine.'

Her brother scowled, and got up from the table. 'If you'd married Matt, and had a couple of kids, you wouldn't be talking that way. It's—it's ungodly!'

'Oh, really!' Olivia found it difficult to contain her anger. So far as Andrew, and her father, were concerned, a woman only had one role in life. And if she deviated from that role, she was both selfish and wicked.

'Anyway, I've got to be getting on,' said Andrew, placing his chair squarely against the table. 'Some of us have work to do.'

Olivia rode the jab. 'All right,' she said, cradling her cup in her hands, and looking up at him over its rim. 'I may come and join you later. Where is everyone, by the way? Sara's bed was empty when I woke up. I thought she'd be down here.'

'I dare say she's about somewhere,' replied Andrew reluctantly. 'I heard Mum say she was going to gather some vegetables, and I think Sara went with her. Why don't you go and join them? They probably need your help more than I do.'

'Oh, Andy!' His almost childish desire to get his own back broke through Olivia's reserve. Unable to sustain her anger against him, she got up from the table, and ignoring his instinctive withdrawal, she gave him a swift hug. 'We've got to forget the past,' she told him gently, looking into hazel eyes that were several shades darker than her own. 'I have missed you—all of you—terribly. But—well, there were reasons why I couldn't come back before now. Please—believe me.'

Andrew's sun-browned features were wary. 'Don't think you can get round me, the way you got round Dad,' he exclaimed, but she could sense he was weakening. 'Oh—all right,' he muttered. 'I missed you, too. But that doesn't mean I forgive you for staying away so long.'

He left, after bestowing a rather awkward kiss on her cheek, and Olivia gave a wistful smile as she seated herself at the table again. Slowly but surely, she told herself firmly. Eventually they would all come round. They were her family, weren't they? And in spite of everything, they loved her. She had to believe that.

Which was more than could be said about her grandmother, she thought ruefully. It was obvious where Harriet Stoner's loyalties had lain, and they had not been with Olivia. She had been a potent reason to stay away from Lower Mychett. So long as Harriet Stoner was alive, Olivia would always have felt the outsider, the cuckoo in the nest.

Not that she could totally blame her grandmother for that, Olivia admitted. And, in all fairness, she had not been the only reason Olivia had stayed away. Her dread of seeing Matthew again, of rekindling all the pain and anguish she had felt at leaving, had provided a far more powerful deterrent. And she had been right to take those precautions, she conceded uneasily. Even now, the chemistry was still active, and avoidance seemed the only cure.

CHAPTER FOUR

A SHADOW darkened the open doorway, and Olivia, who had been lost in thought, looked up almost guiltily. She was so used to being active. The agency she had founded, and which she now ran with the help of an American woman, Agnes Reina, demanded a lot of her energy, and it was rare that she found time to simply sit and meditate. Consequently, there was a look almost of culpability in her eyes when she turned her head, and the man in the doorway raised his eyebrows enquiringly.

'All alone?' he asked, propping his shoulder against the jamb, and surveying her intently. 'What's the matter? Has someone been upsetting you?'

Olivia's nerves jangled. In tight jeans and a cotton shirt, that was open part-way down his chest, Matthew looked even more attractive today than he had done yesterday. His dark hair was ruffled, as if he had used his fingers instead of a comb, and his cool grey eyes were narrowed and disturbing.

'No more than usual,' Olivia answered at last, having taken a few moments to get her reactions to him under control. It wouldn't do to let him see how he unsettled her. And she was realising, belatedly, that by agreeing to stay on after her grandmother's funeral she was committing herself to more than just a family reconciliation.

'What's that supposed to mean?' he asked now, pushing himself away from the door, and stepping into the room. 'What have they been saying? Talk to me. I want to know.'

Olivia looked away from his demanding gaze. 'Why should you care?' she countered, picking up her coffee-cup again, only to find it was empty. *Damn*, she thought impatiently, pushing the cup aside. She would have welcomed having something to do with her hands. But she wasn't going to attempt to refill it. Not with Matthew watching her, and her nerves governing her movements.

'I don't know—but I do,' Matthew responded evenly, swinging out a chair from the table, straddling it, and folding his arms along the back. 'That's why I came over, actually. I thought I'd better come and see if you needed any support.'

'No. No support needed,' said Olivia jerkily, and, unable to sit still under his calm appraisal, she got to her feet. Then, picking up the pot of coffee, she carried it busily to the sink, taking off the lid and pouring its contents down the drain.

She did it carelessly, recklessly, and the hot coffee splashed up over her hands, causing her to catch her breath. 'Damn,' she said audibly this time, and Matthew swung himself off the chair, and came to see what she had done.

'It's nothing,' she said, flustered by his nearness, and by the way her skin prickled every time she looked at him. She thrust her hands behind her back. 'Go and sit down. I'll make some more coffee. I'm sure that's what my mother would expect me to do.'

'There was nothing wrong with that coffee,' commented Matthew drily, putting his hand behind her, and drawing her resisting fingers towards him. 'Here,' he said, his lips compressing when he saw the red marks that marred her pale skin. Turning on the cold tap, he forced her hand under its cooling spray and she immediately felt its relief. 'Now, do you want to tell me what's going on?'

'Nothing's going on,' protested Olivia, the pressure of his hard fingers on her wrist causing a burning sensation to run up her arm. 'Honestly, everyone's been very—nice.'

'Nice?'

Matthew looked down at her with darkening eyes, and Olivia's breathing got shallower and shallower. 'Yes—nice,' she repeated, dragging her eyes away, and con-

centrating on the stream of water spilling over her hand.
'I'm not saying we haven't had our moments——'

'I'll bet.' Matthew pulled her hand towards him, and
after discovering that the marks were much less angry
he turned off the tap. But he didn't release her, and Olivia
prayed no one would come in and find them like this.
'I know what your old man can be like,' he continued,
tearing off a sheet of kitchen towel and dabbing her hand
dry. 'Remember how he used to chivvy me about driving
too fast when you were in the car?'

'Mmm.'

Olivia forced a polite smile, and finally succeeded in
pulling her hand away. But when she moved across the
room, on the pretext of collecting the dirty cups from
the table, Matthew came after her.

'Do you mind?' she said, when she turned with the
cups in her hands, and found him right behind her. 'I
want to wash these up.'

Matthew hesitated, and for one awful moment she
thought he was going to touch her again. And she didn't
know how she would react if he did. Drop the cups
probably, she thought unsteadily, and that would be the
least of her worries.

But the problem didn't arise. Matthew's hesitation was
only momentary. Then, he inclined his head and stepped
aside, saying, as he did so, 'What are you going to do
today?'

'Today?' Olivia carried the dishes to the sink, and
turned on the taps, giving herself time to absorb his
question. 'Um—I don't know,' she said nervously,
wishing he would go. 'Whatever's necessary, I suppose.
There must be something I can do. I'm not completely
helpless.'

'Did I say you were?'

Matthew came to rest his hips against the drainer
beside her, and Olivia's temperature sky-rocketed. Dear
God, she thought, after the things he had said to her the
day before, she hadn't expected to see him again. Not
alone, anyway. She would probably have seen him at the

funeral, she conceded, but surely then he would be with his wife. *His wife* . . .

'Where—er—where's Helen?' she asked, ignoring his question, and wishing either her mother, or Sara, or even Mrs Davis, would appear. Why was it that when you needed someone most they never came?

'I don't know.' Matthew answered her without rancour. Then, without missing a beat, 'Who's been saying you're helpless?'

'Oh, *Matt*!' Olivia couldn't sustain the prolonged drain upon her emotional resources and, leaving the dishes, she wiped her hands on a teacloth and moved away. Then, keeping her back to him, she lifted her hands and gripped the back of her neck, before saying painfully, 'What are you doing here, Matt? I thought we had nothing to say to one another!'

'Did I say that?'

'Stop asking questions you know the answers to,' she exclaimed frustratedly, and she heard the sigh he gave, before hurrying on, 'I—I want you to go, Matt. I don't think it's a good idea for us to see one another again.'

'Why not?'

His voice was low and husky, its rich timbre overlaid by a veneer of coolness, but sexy none the less. God, it reminded her of the way he had spoken to her when he was making love to her, she thought unsteadily, his voice like thick velvet stroking her senses, while his hands . . .

But it was *wrong*, she flayed herself desperately. She had to stop thinking of Matthew in those terms. And if she couldn't tell him the real reason, she could at least remind him of his responsibilities.

'Because you're married,' she said, schooling her features as she turned to face him. And then, realising how revealing the silk vest was, she crossed her hands over her chest. 'I—I think you should go.'

'What if I don't want to?' he countered, using his hands to propel himself away from the drainer, and coming towards her, and Olivia put out a warning hand.

'Matt——'

'Oh, Matt, it's you!'

Olivia had never been so relieved to hear the sound of her mother's voice before. Felicity Stoner wheeled herself into the kitchen from the garden, helped only minimally by her younger daughter, and Matthew was obliged to turn towards her. His dark face took on an expression of warm approval, and watching him Olivia wondered at his capacity for deceit. Was she responsible for that, too, or was she only fooling herself by thinking he was masking his real feelings?

'Hello, Fliss,' he said, bending to give her mother a kiss on the cheek. 'How are you?' He gave her a critical look. 'You're looking good.'

Olivia's mother responded predictably, her pale cheeks colouring at the easy compliment. 'I'm sure I look every one of my fifty-odd years,' she retorted, patting his hand affectionately. 'I won't say exactly how many odd years. I'd rather not remember I'm getting old.'

'Well, you don't look a day over forty,' Matthew assured her, his smile shifting to include the woman behind the wheelchair in its warmth. 'How are you, Sara? When's the new arrival due?'

'At the end of September.' Sara blossomed under his scrutiny, and Olivia felt a cold hand squeeze her stomach. If only she had been the Stoners' *younger* daughter, she thought enviously. She and Matthew——

'Have you made Matt some coffee, Olivia?' her mother was asking now, and, forcing herself to concentrate on the present and not the past, she ruefully shook her head.

'No.'

'No?' Mrs Stoner looked impatient. 'Oh, Olivia, why not? Do you want him to think we're totally inhospitable?'

'No, I——'

'I don't think Liv cares what I think,' remarked Matthew lazily, though when he looked in Olivia's direction his eyes were anything but lazy. They glittered with a disturbing defiance, and she was very much afraid she was going to regret crossing swords with him.

'Oh, Matt, I'm sure that's not true,' exclaimed Mrs Stoner, but the look she cast at her elder daughter was anxious. 'Olivia—you haven't been having words with Matt, have you? I hoped—well, after all these years, I hoped you two might be friends!'

'Oh, Mum——'

Olivia felt as if she was being torn to pieces. Surely her mother must know what she was asking, and yet she could sit there, looking so incredibly innocent, when if it hadn't been for her she and Matthew might have been married now...

'We are friends.' For reasons best known to himself, Matthew chose to relieve Olivia's anguish, and she gazed at him helplessly as he gave her a teasing smile. But the teasing didn't reach his eyes, she noticed. They were just as challenging; just as full of defiance.

'Are you?'

Mrs Stoner did not look totally convinced, but, as usual with her, she chose not to pursue it. Was that the way her mother had lived with herself all these years? Olivia wondered. By deluding herself that what was blatantly obvious was not necessarily the way it was?

Olivia turned away to put on the kettle, and spoon several measures of the aromatic grains into the coffee-filter. She supposed she should feel angry with her mother, but she never had. How could you blame someone who had suffered so much pain in her life already? If Felicity Stoner had deluded herself that Olivia's leaving home had had nothing to do with her own betrayal, then so be it. Some might say she had paid in other ways for what might have been a single indiscretion.

'So, what are you doing here, Matt?' Mrs Stoner was asking now, and Olivia listened tensely for his reply. After all, she didn't even know where he lived any more, or how he spent his time.

'Well, as a matter of fact, I came to see if Liv would like to come to Abbot's Norton with me,' he said, causing Olivia to spill coffee grains all over the drainer. 'I've got to see Peabody at the bank, and buy a couple of plugs for Aldridge. One of the tractors started playing up yesterday, and I promised I'd call in at Fennings, while I was in town.'

'I see.' Felicity Stoner cast a doubtful glance at her daughter's determinedly unyielding back. 'How kind of you! Well—I'm sure Olivia would appreciate the chance to reacquaint herself with all her old haunts. I mean, there've been quite a lot of changes, haven't there? Not least that indoor shopping mall they've built, where the old bus station used to be——'

'It *is* kind of you, Matt, but I can't go,' said Olivia abruptly, realising she was the only one likely to make a stand on her behalf. She swung round, with the coffee-pot in her hand, her face schooled into an expression of polite regret. 'I—er—I only arrived yesterday, as you know, and I haven't really had a chance yet to be with the family. There were so many people here when I arrived, and tomorrow it's the funeral, and——'

'But you're not leaving after the funeral, are you, darling?' her mother protested artlessly, and Olivia heard Matthew's sudden intake of breath. 'I know your grandmother's death has been a great shock to all of us, and I'm sure you feel as if you ought to stay here and do what you can, but it's really not necessary. You'd be amazed how much I can do, and there's Mrs Davis, and Sara, of course.' She gave her younger daughter a warm smile. 'I think it would be altogether better if you went with Matt: got some fresh air; made an effort to catch up on old times. We can manage. And after the funeral's over, we'll have plenty of time to—talk.'

Olivia wondered if she only imagined her mother's hesitation before the word 'talk', but now was not the time to consider it. Taking a steadying breath, her gaze flickered briefly over Matthew's dark, enigmatic face, before settling on the coffee-pot she was holding. 'And what if I don't *want* to go?' she asked, and she could hear the rising note of anxiety in her voice. 'Perhaps—perhaps—*Helen*—might like to go with—with her husband.' She lifted her head and looked at him. 'Where did you say Helen was, Matt? I'm afraid I can't remember.'

If she had thought to disconcert him, she was wrong, although she sensed he was not pleased by her enquiry. Even her mother looked a little discomfited now, but it was Sara, seated rather inelegantly at the kitchen table, who said carelessly, 'Haven't you told Livvy about Helen, Matt?' She arched her brows sardonically. 'Helen spends all her time with her precious horses,' she added, for her sister's benefit. 'You remember the Berrenger Stables, don't you, Livvy? Since her father died, Helen practically runs the place single-handed.'

Olivia exchanged a look with Matthew. 'Helen's father's dead?' she asked in surprise. To her recollection, Conrad Berrenger had been younger than her father.

'Yes.' Matthew's response was curt, but Sara was evidently relishing holding centre stage.

'He was killed, when he was out hunting,' she exclaimed, as Felicity Stoner made a sound of protest. 'It caused quite a scandal. The coroner said it was accidental death, but the rumours were flying around that he was in debt up to——'

'I think that will do, Sara.' Mrs Stoner's usually placid features were agitated now, but her younger daughter only arched her brows expressively.

'Well, I'm sorry, but it's only what people said at the time,' she protested. 'I mean, everyone thought he would have to sell, didn't they, Matt?' she added, appealing to him, and Matt said,

'Perhaps so,' in a flat, dispassionate voice.

'Sara, it's not your business!' exclaimed Mrs Stoner, her cheeks pink with embarrassment, her hands tight around the arms of her chair. 'I don't know what Matt must be thinking, listening to you discussing his private

affairs like this!' She expelled her breath noisily, before
continuing, 'And Olivia, are you going to make some
coffee, or aren't you? You're standing there holding that
jug as if you didn't know what to do with it!'

Olivia pulled herself together with an effort, and
turned to put the coffee-pot under the filter. She had
been acting as if she'd lost the use of her limbs, she
thought ruefully, but in spite of all the years that had
passed since she went away her mother could still ex-
ercise a daunting authority. Nevertheless, Sara's revelations about the Berrengers had aroused her curiosity.
Conrad Berrenger had been such a strong, active man,
and an excellent rider. It was hard to believe he had died
in such circumstances. Yet the alternative was equally
unpalatable. Although her sister hadn't actually put the
rumour into words, her meaning had been clear enough.
Helen's father had obviously been suspected of having
committed suicide, leaving, no doubt, a hefty insurance
policy to settle all his debts.

'I'm sorry, Matt,' her mother was apologising now,
but Matthew merely gave a careless shrug of his shoulder.

'It's not important,' he said, clearly wishing they could
change the conversation. 'It's not as if it's news, Fliss.
And Liv was bound to hear the gossip sooner or later.'

'Even so——' Felicity Stoner shook her head. 'I still
say Sara shouldn't have said what she did.' She looked
at her younger daughter reprovingly. 'If this is what
having a baby does for you, I'm surprised Jeff allows
you to stay on the base!'

'Oh, Mum!' Sara pulled a face. 'I'm not a child, you
know. And you heard what Matt said—Livvy was bound
to hear about the Berrengers from someone.'

'Matt was only being polite,' retorted her mother,
propelling her wheelchair to the table, and tapping her
nails against the wood. 'Now, where are those peas we
picked earlier? I'll shell them, while Olivia makes the
coffee.'

Olivia, meanwhile, couldn't make up her mind whether
it was Sara or their mother who had made the situation

so uncomfortable. Sara probably shouldn't have said anything, it was true, but if Mrs Stoner hadn't chosen to take her up on it their present state of antagonism with one another would not have been so obvious.

Looking at Matthew, she felt a sudden—and un-welcome—rush of compassion. It wasn't as if he needed her sympathy, she told herself, trying to dismiss the feeling out of hand. But the fact remained, she did feel some affiliation with him, and when he caught her eyes upon him she didn't look away.

Of course, eventually, she had to. The kettle was boiling, and needed attention, and she didn't trust Sara not to notice what was going on and make her own as-sessment about it. Not that anything was going on, she chided herself severely. For a few moments, she and Matthew had looked at one another without animosity, that was all. And wasn't that what she should be striving for? A casual relationship with him, without any sexual undertones.

'Are you coming to town?' he asked abruptly, as Olivia turned to set cups and saucers, cream and sugar, on the table. And, before she could think of a single reason why not, her mother butted in.

'Of course she is,' she said, taking the coffee-pot from her daughter's unresisting fingers, and filling one of the generously sized cups. 'There's nothing for her to do here, Matt. We're all just marking time until tomorrow. It'll be easier on all of us, when Gran is laid to rest. Then we can get on with our own lives, instead of thinking about the past.'

Olivia stiffened. 'Mum——'

'Drink your coffee, dear,' directed Mrs Stoner imper-turbably, pushing the cups across the table. 'There you are, Matt. Would you like a biscuit? Olivia wouldn't think to offer you one. I've noticed she hardly eats enough to keep a fly alive.'

Matthew took the cup of coffee, but he refused one of the home-baked ginger creams Mrs Stoner brought from the pantry. 'This is fine,' he said, his eyes on her

elder daughter as if waiting for her response. And, realising it was going to be simpler just to let her mother
have her way, Olivia sighed.

'All right,' she answered. 'I'll go with you. And
perhaps Sara would like to come, too.'

Matthew's eyes darkened at this suggestion, but once
again it was Olivia's mother who had the last word. 'Oh,
I don't think so, dear,' she said, before her younger
daughter could respond to the invitation. 'I don't think
Matt would appreciate being seen about Abbot's Norton
with a pregnant woman in tow. I mean,' she added disarmingly, treating Sara to a beguiling smile, 'I don't have
to tell you how people talk, do I? Particularly after what
you said about the Berrengers.'

CHAPTER FIVE

ABBOT'S NORTON was fairly quiet on this late August morning. On market days, the small town brimmed with people, and it was scarcely possible to move along its narrow, crowded streets. But today it was easy to drive into the market place, easy to find somewhere to park. Which was just as well, thought Olivia. The dark green Range Rover Matthew was driving wouldn't fit into the smallest of spaces.

The journey from Lower Mychett had been accomplished in a little over twenty minutes. Although it was only fifteen miles, the roads were narrow, and at this time of the year there were a lot of tractors clogging the lanes, loaded down with hay and other silage.

They hadn't talked much on the way. In keeping with her determination to keep her relationship with Matthew as casual as possible, Olivia had made some superficial comments about harvesting, and the weather, but nothing of a controversial nature. And Matthew had responded in kind, keeping his attention firmly fixed on the road ahead.

But now, with the Range Rover securely lodged in the new multi-storey car park, they were both free to follow their own pursuits, and, looping the strap of her handbag over one shoulder, Olivia gave her escort what she hoped was a bracing smile.

'Well,' she said, as they emerged from the stairwell into the sunlight, 'what time shall we meet to go back?'

'Meet?' As she half turned away to look up and down Broad Street, Matthew caught her arm. 'What do you mean—*meet*?' he asked, his grey eyes narrowed and intense. 'You're coming with me.'

'Oh, I don't think so.' Olivia looked pointedly down at his hand on her arm, and couldn't suppress a shiver. His skin was so dark against her fairer flesh, and she had a sudden image of how they had looked, naked together... Dear God! She swallowed convulsively. Why did she have to think of *that* now?

'Well, I think so,' said Matthew, but, meeting her tight-lipped gaze, he released her arm. 'I thought you could come with me to the bank, and then we can have some lunch together——'

'No.'

'Why not?'

'Because——' Olivia took a deep breath, searching for a suitable excuse, and found one. 'Well—because, as my mother said, people talk. How do you think it will look if you and I are seen having lunch together?'

'I don't particularly care,' replied Matthew, in a low, charged tone, and Olivia took an involuntary step back from him.

'Well—well, I do,' she said, shocked by his vehemence. 'I—don't understand. Yesterday, you said we couldn't be friends—— '

'Friends!' Matthew used the word like a curse. 'Who said anything about being friends? The way I feel about you has nothing to do with friendship!'

'Matt——'

She would have turned away again, but he stepped in front of her, imprisoning her against the wall of the car park, with one hand at either side of her head. 'I mean it,' he said, though there was no trace of warmth in his face. 'I actually find I can't keep away from you, isn't that a laugh? When I woke up this morning, all I could think about was coming over to the farm to see you.'

'Oh, Matt——'

Olivia turned her head aside, afraid to look into his eyes, in case he saw something in hers she didn't want him to see. Besides, she was uneasily aware of how dangerous her present situation was. She had only to look up at him, only to raise herself a few inches, to

touch his mouth with hers. And the awful need to do
so was tearing her apart.

Along the street, people were going about their daily
lives, unaware of the aching tumult in hers. Women
wheeling prams; couples with young children; old people,
enjoying the uncharacteristically long dry spell; all went
by without more than a passing glance. And, fortunately, none of them recognised Matthew, she thought
unsteadily. Because all his attention was concentrated
on her, and everyone knew that Matthew Ryan was
married to someone else...

'What's the matter?' he demanded now, his warm
breath fanning her cheek. 'Don't pretend it doesn't give
you a kick, knowing you've got me over a barrel! How
does it feel to know someone wants you so badly that
they're prepared to make a fool of themselves all over
again?'

Olivia couldn't take any more. Before he realised what
she was going to do, she ducked under his arm, and
hurried off along Broad Street. Then, realising he was
following her, she darted into a women's clothes shop.
It was comparatively easy to hide herself among the many
racks of skirts and dresses, and, just to reassure the store
detective that she wasn't a shoplifter, she carried a pair
of trousers into the fitting-room.

The trousers didn't fit, but then she had hardly
expected them to. She had just picked them haphazardly
off the rail, and they were several sizes too large. She
felt a bit of a fool, trying them on, but with other eyes
watching her she felt obliged to make the effort. After
all, she had probably drawn suspicion to herself by
carrying them into the changing-room in the first place.
Still, she had done nothing wrong, so there was really
no need for her to feel so guilty.

Depositing the cotton trousers on the rejection rail,
she walked outside again with a feeling of relief. It was
good to get out into the sunshine, and away from the
drumming beat of the music that had filled the shop.
But now she would have to find the bus station, or a

taxi rank, to arrange her transportation back to Lower
Mychett. And preferably before Matthew went back, and
told everyone he had lost her.

'Find anything interesting?'

The deep, attractive voice was unmistakable, and
Olivia's head flew round to complete the identification.
Matthew had apparently been waiting outside the shop
all the time, and his unobtrusive enquiry was delivered
in a low, unaggressive tone.

Olivia sighed. 'No,' she said, having no choice but to
allow him to fall into step beside her. 'They didn't have
another exit.'

Matthew absorbed this silently for a few minutes, and
then, when they paused at the intersection with Cannon
Street, he said, 'OK. You've made your point. You didn't
really want to come with me, and you're not interested
in my invitation to lunch. So—what do you want to do?
Go off on your own?'

Olivia pressed her lips together. Matthew was looking
tired now, and once again sympathy for him almost
overwhelmed her. She badly wanted to tell him that she'd
like nothing better than to have lunch with him, but
common sense prevailed, and she forced herself to nod.

'That—sounds good to me,' she said, glancing up at
him and away. 'We—er—we could meet back at the car
park, at say—half-past twelve. What do you think? Will
that give you plenty of time to do what you have to do?'

'Ample,' he conceded flatly, and then another voice
spoke his name.

'Matt! Matthew,' exclaimed a young attractive brunette, with a pushchair in tow, stopping right in front
of them. 'I thought it was you. It's been ages since we've
seen you. Where have you been hiding yourself? Why
don't you ever accept my invitations?'

'Oh—hello, Julie.' Olivia thought Matthew was less
than enthusiastic about the unexpected intervention.
'How are you? How's David?'

'We're fine.' Julie gave him a warm smile, and then
turned to give Olivia a speculative look. 'I know you,

don't I? You're one of the Stoner girls, aren't you?' she added, rather patronisingly. 'I assume you must be the one who didn't go to America.'

'No, I——'

'Olivia is home from the States for her grandmother's funeral,' broke in Matthew, running his hand through the thick dark hair at his nape. 'Liv,' his eyes were wary, 'you remember Julie Redding, don't you? She used to come to Rycroft to play tennis. Her mother and mine went to school together.'

'It's Julie Moreton now,' the brunette declared, regarding Olivia with undisguised curiosity. Her eyes flickered from her to Matthew, and back again, before she continued, 'Oh, yes. You two used to know each other—quite well, didn't you. Before Matthew married Helen, of course.'

Her implication was plain, and, in spite of all the reasons why she shouldn't care, Olivia found she did. The implication was that Matthew had only been marking time with her until he and Helen could tie the knot. Any serious relationship between them had never been on the cards.

'Matt and I are—old friends,' Olivia declared now, and the way she said it left Julie in no doubt as to the veracity of that statement. She gave the woman a determinedly pleasant smile. 'Unfortunately, I had to go away to work, but I'm hoping to renew our acquaintance.'

She ignored Matthew's shocked reaction, ignored the fact that she was treading into water far deeper than any she had plumbed this far. The desire to wipe the smug smile from Julie Moreton's face had taken precedence, and judging by the other woman's expression she was succeeding.

'Well,' said Julie tightly, 'how interesting. Funerals do bring together the most unlikely people.'

'Don't they?'

How Olivia stopped herself from saying something completely outrageous, she never knew, but Julie evidently saw the danger, and drew back. 'So, Matt,' she said, addressing herself to him exclusively, 'it's been lovely to see you again. I'll be sure and tell David all about it. It's just a pity you're not alone. We could have shared a sandwich together, and talked about old times.' She looked down at the baby, napping in his pushchair. 'Petey doesn't need feeding again for hours, and——'

'Well——' began Matthew, but this time Olivia had to speak.

'It is a pity,' she said, sliding her arm around Matthew's and holding on. The muscle in his arm stiffened beneath her fingers, but she ignored it, looking up at him deliberately and producing a disarming smile. 'But we're going to the Crown, aren't we, Matt? For old times' sake, hmm? And it's not really the sort of place to take—Petey, was it?'

She said the name disparagingly, even though she had no quarrel with the baby, sleeping in his pushchair. It wasn't his fault that his mother chose to call him by such an absurd diminutive. But she was so angry that she could have screamed, and she would have said anything to end this encounter.

However, it wasn't until Julie had said her goodbyes and walked away that the enormity of what she had done really struck her. She had embarrassed Matthew in front of a friend of his wife's, and implied a relationship between them that she was trying to forget.

'Are you crazy?'

It was Matthew who took the offensive now, and Olivia let go of his arm to sweep the weight of her hair back from her face. 'I—didn't realise your invitation to lunch had to be kept a secret,' she exclaimed, but the indignation in her voice was hardly convincing.

'It didn't,' he retorted, and, realising they were blocking the footpath, Matthew gripped her upper arm and urged her across the street. 'But, in case you've forgotten, you turned me down.' His lips twisted. 'And, before Julie came on the scene, I got the distinct impression you were trying to avoid me!'

'Matt——'

'No, you listen to me. I don't know what sort of game you're playing, but, I'm warning you, don't play with fire! If you'd wanted me, you'd never have left the village, and I won't have you implying anything else, just because it suits you!'

'You don't know what I wanted,' declared Olivia rashly, wrenching her arm away from his biting grasp. 'Oh—I'll see you later,' she added, massaging the red marks he had left on her flesh. 'Let's make it a quarter to one, shall we? To allow for the time we've wasted——'

'Let's not,' countered Matthew, once again blocking her escape. 'As you've told Julie we're having lunch at the Crown, let's do that, shall we? Or would you rather compound the fiction by chickening out?'

Olivia avoided his eyes. 'She won't know——'

'Julie knows a lot of people here. She might.'

'But——' Olivia felt trapped '—after what you said just now, I'd have thought you wouldn't want us to be seen together.'

'Don't talk rubbish! I brought you into town, didn't I? The least controversial thing we can do is have lunch at the Crown. If we were having an affair, I'd hardly take you there.'

Olivia expelled her breath a little unevenly. An *affair*! Her palms felt damp. 'But—you wanted to go to the bank.'

'I'll go afterwards,' replied Matthew levelly. 'After so much—hot air—what I need right now is a drink.'

The Crown Hotel stood at the end of Broad Street. It had been there for as long as Olivia could remember, and she and Matthew had often sat in its comfortable saloon bar in the old days. There had been wooden booths then, with round tables surrounded on three sides by a cushioned seat, which had been ideal for young couples wanting privacy. They had met there on winter evenings, when it had been too cold to sit in Matthew's car. Until she had decided to take the train up to London, and Matthew had introduced her to the delights of sharing his bed . . .

But she mustn't think of that now, Olivia told herself anxiously, as they entered the imposing entrance hall of the hotel. She had made enough mistakes for one morning, and telling Julie they were lunching here had not been the least of them. This place was too familiar. It held too many memories. And if Matthew sat beside her, in the intimacy of a booth, would she be able to remember that *their* intimacy was now forbidden?

However, her fears on that score were soon dispelled. Like the rest of Abbot's Norton, the Crown had had a facelift, and the dark little booths had been removed. In their place were wrought-iron tables and plush armchairs, presently filled with the lunchtime crowd, enjoying pies and sandwiches with their beer.

Her relief must have shown in her face, because Matthew's eyes narrowed sardonically. 'What's the matter?' he enquired. 'Were you afraid I might be tempted to make a pass at you under the table?'

Olivia coloured. She couldn't help it. But, 'No,' she said, as she followed him to the bar, and requested a glass of white wine. 'I wouldn't expect you to be so crass. We're not teenagers now, you know.'

'I know.' Matthew's voice was terse, as he ordered her white wine, and half a pint of lager for himself. 'I think I had more sense then,' he added, carrying their drinks across to an empty table. 'It was only when you went away that I lost it.'

There was no answer Olivia could make to that, and instead she picked up her drink and tasted it. The wine was cool and clear, and marvellously refreshing, and she put out her tongue to clear her lips of every drop. It was only when she caught Matthew watching her that she realised how provocative her action had been, and in future she made sure she didn't repeat it.

'So,' he said, after she had laboriously inspected every other occupant of the bar besides himself, 'you're not returning to the States after the funeral.'

'What?' Olivia pretended to have been diverted, and patiently he repeated his statement. 'Oh—no. Well, not immediately, anyway,' she amended cautiously. 'My mother wants me to stay on for a little while.'

'And do you?'

'Well, of course.' Olivia lifted her shoulders in a careless gesture. 'It's lovely to see all the family again.'

Matthew's dark brows arched. 'Is it? So why didn't you make the effort to come and see them before this? Why did there have to be a funeral before you came back? Have you been *so* busy making money?'

Olivia caught her breath. 'You have no right to say that to me!' she protested, and after a moment he nodded.

'No,' he conceded heavily. 'No, I don't. I'm sorry. I'm trying to keep this impersonal, but it isn't easy.'

Olivia pressed her lips together. 'You shouldn't always jump to conclusions,' she mumbled, unable to prevent the mild defence. 'Things—things aren't always what they seem.'

'Aren't they?' Matthew was regarding her intently now, and Olivia realised that once again she had spoken rashly. 'Are you saying there were other reasons than the obvious one for why you left home?'

'No!' Olivia had to divert those suspicions at all costs, and, shaking her head, she added, 'I meant—I had my reasons for not coming back.'

'Me?'

'You?' Olivia hid her reaction. 'Um—no. No. Not you. I—I thought my father hadn't forgiven me. And—and I was right.'

'Why? Has he been giving you a hard time?'

Olivia bent her head. 'Not exactly.' She shrugged. 'I'd rather not talk about it.'

'OK. And that was the only reason you didn't come home?'

Olivia nodded. 'Yes.' That, and a grandmother who had warned her it would be wiser to stay away, she appended silently.

For a while after that, Matthew said nothing, and
Olivia was relieved. It was easier for her to just sit and
drink her wine, and watch other people enjoying themselves. Safer, too, she thought wryly. Whenever she
spoke, she created problems for herself.

Eventually, Matthew suggested they move into the
restaurant for lunch, but Olivia held back. 'Couldn't we
just have a sandwich in here?' she asked, not attracted
by a long-drawn-out meal, over which she was sure to
say the wrong thing. 'I'm—er—I'm not very hungry, I'm
afraid.'

'Are you ever?' remarked Matthew sardonically. 'All
right. If that's what you want. They even do a fairly
passable lasagne, if that appeals to you.'

'Um—no. A ham sandwich would be fine,' she assured him firmly. 'And some coffee, if they have it.'

'Oh, I'm sure they have it, but whether you'll like it
is another matter,' commented Matthew drily, getting
up from his chair. 'OK. I won't be a minute.'

When he came back, he was carrying an oval plate
containing an assortment of sandwiches. There was ham,
and cheese, and egg mayonnaise, and Olivia regarded
them with real enthusiasm. They had obviously been
freshly made, and the smell of new bread was irresistible.

'She'll bring the coffee in a few minutes,' remarked
Matthew, seating himself again. 'Help yourself.'

And Olivia did so, biting into a crisp roll with more
enjoyment than she had shown for any food in years.
She was sure it was butter on the bread, and Perry, who
was a fanatic about saturated fats, would probably have
a fit if he knew what she was doing. But he didn't. Only
Matthew was a witness to her transgression, and he was
just as bad, munching a cheese and tomato sandwich
with an obvious lack of concern.

'Good, hmm?' he said, unaware of her ambivalence,
and Olivia cast caution to the wind.

'Very good,' she agreed, helping herself to another
roll. 'I'd forgotten what real bread tastes like.
Perry——'

She broke off abruptly, annoyed with herself for bringing Perry's name into it, but Matthew's eyes barely flickered before he asked, 'Perry? Is that the man you live with?'

'I don't *live* with him!' Olivia found herself correcting his assumption, even though it would probably have been better if he had thought she did. 'We—I—have my own apartment. But he is a close friend, yes.'

Matthew studied her. 'I understand he set you up in business,' he said quietly. 'Did he really do that for nothing?'

'He didn't—set me up in business,' replied Olivia steadily. '*I* got the idea for starting the agency for British nannies in New York. Perry—helped me to get finance, that's all.' She sniffed. 'Anyway, I don't know why I'm telling you this. It's nothing to do with you.'

'No.' Matthew conceded the point. But after a moment, he asked, 'Where did you meet him, then? He doesn't sound the type to mix with the Stephen Kramers of this world.'

'What would you know about it?' exclaimed Olivia, stung in spite of herself. 'But, if you must know, we met while I was looking after the children of a South American diplomat. Surprisingly enough, I'm good with children—other people's children,' she amended quickly. 'When—when the Kramers came back to England, I went to work for the Martinezes. End of story.'

'End of story, beginning of—what?' enquired Matthew sardonically, but Olivia turned her head away, and the conversation lapsed.

But eventually Matthew spoke again, and when he did so, Olivia endeavoured to equal his objectivity.

'Tell me,' he said, 'what does Perry do to make a living?' And when her eyes sparkled dangerously, he added, 'Really. I'm interested. As—a friend if you like. Someone who—cares about you.'

Olivia stiffened. 'Matt——'

'What?'

His expression was unreadable, and, although she had no real desire to talk about Perry, at least it was a safe topic. All the same, she wished she had never got into this situation. Talking about Perry to Matthew didn't seem right somehow.

Now, she rubbed the pad of her thumb along her lip, wiping away an errant crumb of her sandwich, as she considered how to reply. 'He—he's involved with the stock market,' she said at last, hoping that would satisfy him. 'Um—when do you think she'll bring the coffee?'

'Soon.' Matthew was indifferent. 'So he's a stockbroker, is he? Does he work on Wall Street?'

'No.' Olivia caught her lower lip between her teeth. 'He—invests in things. In—people; and commodities.'

'A commodities broker?'

'No.' This was far more difficult that she'd thought it would be. 'I've told you. He's an investor.'

'And that's a living?'

Matthew's tone was contemptuous now, and Olivia sprang to Perry's defence. 'Well, you can't talk,' she exclaimed. 'You've never had to work for anything in your life. Not really. I don't know what you're doing now, but when I went away you weren't exactly being forced to go to college!'

Matthew's nostrils flared. 'You—don't know anything about my life,' he intoned quietly, but Olivia wasn't prepared to let it rest.

'Then tell me,' she taunted. 'Tell me what you're doing now. As far as I can see, nothing's changed. The Ryans are still the wealthiest family in the district.'

'It depends what you mean by wealthy,' retorted Matthew, and then was silent for a moment, as the waitress set a tray of coffee and two cups on the table. 'We still own the land—or most of it,' he amended. 'But there have been expenses. Not least, the fact that my father made some rather doubtful investments, and lost a lot of money.'

Olivia moistened her lips. 'I see.' She paused. 'Well, I'm sorry. I didn't know that, of course. But, even so——'

'Even so, nothing,' said Matthew flatly. 'The fact is, I'm running the estate on a hand-to-mouth basis. It's going to take us the best part of five years to get back on an even keel. Always providing we have decent summers, of course. Otherwise, we're going to have to sell some of the farms.'

Olivia blinked. '*You're* running the estate?' she echoed.

'Trying to,' conceded Matthew, taking another sandwich.

'But—what about your father?'

Olivia had spoken automatically, but now she put down her half-eaten sandwich and took a deep breath. *Matthew's father!* She had wondered how long it would be before she would have to cope with thinking about Matthew's father, and the role he had played in her life.

'Oh, my father spends most of his time in the estate office,' answered Matthew, unaware of her ambivalence. 'Since Hetherington retired——'

'Mr Hetherington's retired?' It didn't seem possible. The old man had seemed a permanent fixture at Rycroft.

'Well, he was sixty-eight,' said Matthew mildly. 'Anyway, with our financial situation being what it is, it didn't seem sensible to hire another bailiff. Not when Father said he was perfectly capable of doing the job himself.'

Olivia shook her head. 'And—and your mother?'

'She manages,' said Matthew drily. 'We all manage. We have to, don't we?'

And Helen? she wanted to ask, but she didn't have that right. From what Sara had said, Helen didn't care about Rycroft, only about the Berrenger estate. She had always been mad on horses, and apparently she hadn't changed. And now that her father was dead...

CHAPTER SIX

OLIVIA was fourteen when she first got to know Matthew Ryan. Really know him, that was; as in speak to him.

She had known of his existence, of course, for as long as she could remember. She had often seen him in the village, either riding with his mother, or sitting beside his father in the big black Bentley they used to run in those days. Everyone knew about the Ryans. How Matthew's grandfather had died at Dunkirk and how his father had married Lady Lavinia Stacey, the débutante of the season, and brought her to live at Rycroft, soon after the war. They were a constant source of gossip, and Olivia wouldn't have been human if she hadn't listened to some of it.

All the girls in the village talked about Matthew Ryan. From the time he was old enough to be noticed he had become the favourite topic of speculation, and Olivia's friends used to chatter excitedly every time he chanced to look in their direction.

Not that he seemed to notice. Unlike his father, who everyone used to say 'had an eye for the ladies', Matthew had always seemed indifferent to the interest he evoked. He was a solemn child, grey-eyed, and studious. It wasn't until he was older that he had become less serious.

Jenny Mason's mother would say he was like that because his parents were so much older, and he was an only child. She said that the Ryans had been married more than a dozen years before Matthew was born. Indeed, she had added, people had been beginning to say that, for all his philandering ways, old Matt Ryan couldn't sire a son. But then Matthew had come along, the apple of his parents' eye, and all the gossips had been silenced.

Even so, she said, Lady Lavinia had had to go away to have the baby, and because she had had such a hard time the doctors had advised her not to have any more children. In consequence, Matthew had grown up alone, without any brothers and sisters, and Olivia hadn't envied him, living in that big house, without another child to play with.

Until he was thirteen, Matthew had attended the local preparatory school, which also set him apart from the village children. Then, later on, he was sent away to Winchester, and it was only during the holidays that he came back. Olivia had thought it couldn't be very pleasant to be sent away from home either. She knew how much she would miss her family if that had happened to her. Even though, since Sara was born, her grandmother had taken charge of the household, her mother was always there to comfort her, if things became too tough.

For Harriet Stoner had always had little time for her eldest granddaughter. Olivia was expected to spend her free time either helping about the house, or babysitting her younger brother and sister. She seldom attended parties or discos, or joined in the social life of the village. It was only on the very rare occasions when she appealed to her mother that she was allowed to have some fun.

And then, one evening, during the summer when she was fourteen, she had rescued Matthew Ryan's dog from the river.

It had all happened quite spontaneously. For once, Olivia had escaped her chores, and the other children, and gone for a walk along the riverbank. It was a dull evening, with overhanging clouds threatening the rain that was to come. Many of the children had gone home early to avoid getting wet, but Olivia was indifferent to the weather. She was simply enjoying her freedom.

It was then that she saw the young retriever, struggling in the reeds that clogged the bank. It looked little more than a puppy, and had probably plunged into the river after a rat, or some other small animal. She didn't know where it had come from, but it was obviously unable to get out. And, if somebody didn't do something soon it was going to drown. Already its struggles were draining its strength.

Without hesitating, Olivia rolled up the legs of her jeans, kicked off her trainers, and waded into the stream after the puppy. In no time at all, the water had soaked her legs to her thighs, but it was summer, and the water wasn't icy.

The young dog seemed to realise she had come to help it, because it made no protest when she reached down and disentangled its legs from the reeds. On the contrary, it nuzzled against her gratefully, its little heart beating at twice its normal pace.

Cuddling the dog against her, Olivia was wading out of the water when a voice accosted her. 'Hey,' it called. 'Where are you going with that dog? He doesn't belong to you.'

Olivia turned, half indignantly, to face her accuser, and then felt her face deepen with colour when she saw Matthew Ryan standing on the opposite bank. In jeans, and a cotton sweatshirt, he could have been any one of the village youths. Except that he was taller, and darker, and his attitude set him apart.

'I'm not stealing him, if that's what you think,' she called back, as the puppy licked the underside of her jaw. 'If he's your dog, you should look after him. He was tangled in the reeds.'

'Was he?'

Matthew didn't sound convinced, and Olivia's temper flared.

'Yes, he was,' she shouted back, forgetting for a moment who she was talking to. 'You don't think I'd walk into the water with my clothes on for nothing, do you?' She gestured at her wet jeans. 'My gran's going to be furious!'

Matthew's expression grew less accusing. 'Was he really trapped in the reeds?' he asked doubtfully. 'He ran off while I was trying to teach him to walk to heel. Stupid mutt!'

'Well, he was nearly a dead mutt,' retorted Olivia, as the puppy recovered its strength and began to squirm against her. 'How do you want to get him back? Shall I walk into the village, and you can meet me at the bridge?'

'I'd rather not.' Matthew bit his lip. 'There's a weir a few yards upstream. If you wouldn't mind walking that far, I could come across and get him.'

Olivia hesitated. She knew the weir he meant, and it was considerably more than 'a few yards' upstream. With the sky getting blacker every minute, it was obviously foolish to go so far. But if she took the dog back to the village, everyone would know what had happened. And for some reason she didn't want that, any more than he did. This was private. Between her and Matthew Ryan. For the first time in her life, she had done something important. Whether she chose to tell Jenny about it later was something she would have to think about.

Matthew evidently mistook her hesitation for something else, and he called, 'I suppose you'd rather go home and change your jeans. I never thought of that, when I said about walking to the weir. And it's going to rain anyway. I'll get the Land Rover, and drive over to your house instead. Where do you live? In the village?'

'No, I—I mean, I don't mind about being wet,' shouted Olivia hastily, imagining how her grandmother would react if she took the puppy home. Of course, she'd probably be very nice while Matthew was there, but after he was gone . . .

'Well, if you're sure.'

'I am.'

Olivia nodded, and started along the bank, clutching the puppy in her arms. So what if it did rain? she thought resignedly. She was wet anyway. One way or another, she was going to rouse her grandmother's wrath.

'What's its name?' she called, as they kept pace with one another, on either side of the river, and Matthew grinned.

'Would you believe—Leander?' he shouted ruefully. 'That's the first part of his name anyway. We call him Sandy, for obvious reasons. But it is rather ironic, don't you think?'

Olivia frowned. 'Why?'

'Oh—well, Hero and Leander are part of Greek mythology. Hero lived on one side of a stretch of water, called the Hellespont, and Leander lived on the other. And every night Leander swam the Hellespont to get to his lover.'

'I see.' Olivia nodded.

'No, you don't. That wasn't the end of the story,' said Matthew wryly. 'One night, a storm blew up, and Leander was drowned! I guess I'll have to watch that little beggar. There may not always be someone around to save him.'

Olivia smiled. It was nice to know he believed her now, and she cast a covert glance in his direction. She could hardly believe what was happening. She was actually having a conversation with Matthew Ryan! The other girls in the village would be green with envy. If she ever told them, she amended thoughtfully. Which wasn't an absolute certainty.

Of course, it did rain, and she did get wet, particularly her trainers, which she had left lying on the bank, while she walked the half-mile or so to the weir barefoot. But it gave her an excuse not to tell anyone else what had happened, and for the next two years she kept the knowledge to herself.

Then, when she was sixteen, she ran into Matthew again. Literally ran into him, this time. She was cycling back from Jenny's house, one snowy February afternoon, when she came round a bend in the road, and found Matthew's car stuck half in the ditch. Not expecting to find anything on the road in these conditions, she was unprepared for the blockage. And as her brakes were wet and slippery, they didn't have much traction.

Even so, she managed to avoid hurting herself too badly, by jumping off the bike before it connected with Matthew's back bumper, and he came round from checking the bonnet to find her sprawled in a drift.

'Hey—aren't you——?'

It was obvious he remembered her, but perhaps not from where, and Olivia was absurdly glad that she was wearing her best blue parka as his grey eyes swiftly swept up and down her body. Tall for her age, Olivia found it rather a novelty to be able to look up at him. The boys of her acquaintance were all under-sized.

But then, Matthew Ryan wasn't a boy, she thought, feeling an unfamiliar surge of excitement. He was nineteen or twenty at least, and he was a student at the university in London.

'Oh—I'm all right,' she said, brushing the remaining specks of snow from her skirt. 'Did you—corner too fast, or something? I could cycle to Pollack's garage, if you need help.'

Matthew grinned, and Olivia's heart turned over. He had such a nice mouth, and his teeth were white and even. It wasn't fair, she thought, that one person should be so attractive. It wasn't just his dark good looks, or the lean, muscled strength of his body. He just seemed a really genuine human being, with a sense of humour to match her own.

'We really should stop meeting like this,' he remarked humorously now, gesturing towards the damp patches on her coat. 'Without you getting soaked to the skin, I mean. And thanks for your offer to ride to the garage. But I think I might be able to get it out myself.'

'I'll help, if you like,' offered Olivia impulsively, aware of a desire to do anything to prolong this encounter. If she was late home, so be it. It wouldn't be the first time she had got into trouble because of him.

'OK.' Matthew regarded her consideringly. 'Can you drive?'

'Drive?' Olivia's voice faltered. How old did he think she was? 'Um—well, I've driven a tractor,' she volunteered doubtfully.

'Well, that's something, I suppose.' Matthew swung open the car door, and indicated that she should get inside. 'I'll explain what I want you to do, then we'll take it from there.'

In the event, Olivia proved an apt pupil, and with Matthew heaving on the rear fender the Mini eventually skidded out on to the road. Its sudden traction caused Matthew to lose his balance this time, and Olivia couldn't stop herself from laughing as she got out of the car. Matthew had sat down in the slush, and the seat of his trousers was soaking.

'I know, I know,' he muttered good-naturedly, examining his trousers as best he could. 'I bet you did that deliberately. It's a wonder I didn't slide down into the ditch.'

Olivia sobered. 'Oh—really, I didn't——' she began, and Matthew grinned again.

'I'm only kidding,' he said, abandoning his efforts to squeeze any water out of his jeans, and turning back to pick up her bicycle. 'I may be wet, but I am grateful. I don't think I could have done it without your help.'

Olivia glowed. There was no other word to describe how his words made her feel. But then Matthew scowled, and her sense of well-being dissipated.

'Is—is something wrong?'

'Mmm.' Matthew swung the bike he had picked up round to face her, and she saw the buckled front wheel. 'Looks as if we've got a problem.'

'You mean I have,' she said ruefully, not needing a crystal ball to anticipate how her grandmother, and her father, would react when they saw the bent wheel. She had been warned about riding in slippery conditions, but it took so long to walk to Jenny's house.

'No, we have,' amended Matthew, squatting down on his haunches to examine the damage. 'You know, I think Sam might be able to straighten this.'

'Do you think so?'

Olivia squatted down beside him, and Matthew shrugged. 'Well, we can give it a go,' he said, looking at her over his shoulder. 'Come on. We'll go and find out.'

Olivia's eyes widened. 'Now?'

'Why not?'

'Um—no reason,' murmured, Olivia, torn between the knowledge that being late was only going to add to her problems, and the undoubted excitement of spending a little more time in his company. 'I—all right.'

The bicycle was secured, half in and half out of the boot, and then Matthew thrust open the passenger door for Olivia to get into the car. In the steamy, confined atmosphere of the Mini, she was intensely conscious of his nearness, but there was little time for misgivings as Matthew rocketed the little car down the road to the village. Clearly the accident he had just averted meant nothing to him. He seemed to regard speed as an essential part of driving, and to Olivia, used to her father's rather more sedate pace, it was marvellously stimulating.

Sam Pollack looked at her strangely as Matthew explained what had happened, and Olivia sighed. The Pollacks serviced the farm machinery, and Sam Pollack knew perfectly well who she was, and how *old* she was. It would be just too embarrassing if he chose to treat her like a child, she thought frustratedly.

But Sam apparently cared more for Matthew's good will than the opportunity to make her feel small, and although he obviously had an opinion he kept it to himself. He agreed that he probably could straighten the wheel, but it would take a couple of days, and he couldn't guarantee success.

'Well, do your best, Sam,' said Matthew, as Olivia's heart sank at the delay. She had hoped that, by some miracle, the bike could have been repaired immediately. As it was, she would have to go home without it and explain what she had done.

'Something wrong?' asked Matthew, as they walked across Pollack's yard to where the Mini was waiting. 'Don't worry. Sam will do a good job. If he can't repair it, he'll put on a new wheel.'

'A new wheel!' Olivia was horrified. 'Oh, but——'

'I'll pay for it, of course,' Matthew added soothingly. 'It was my fault you had the accident. It's the least I can do.'

Olivia shook her head. 'I don't think——'

'I insist,' said Matthew, swinging open his door, as if to get into the car, and then pausing, when he realised Olivia wasn't following his example. 'Come on. I'll run you home.'

Olivia swallowed. 'You will?'

Matthew pulled a face at her. 'Well, it is getting dark,' he pointed out drily. 'You surely don't expect me to leave you to walk back to the farm?'

Olivia still hesitated. 'You know where I live?' she asked, in confusion.

'Of course.' Matthew folded his length into the car, and thrust open her door from inside. 'Get in. It's freezing out there.'

Olivia did so, but cautiously, looking at him with vaguely anxious eyes, and Matthew sighed. 'What did you expect? That I wouldn't know where you lived? Olivia—*Liv*? Can I call you that? I've known all about you, since that summer you pulled my dog out of the river.'

Olivia's father was not best pleased when his daughter arrived home in Matthew's car, but his respect for the Ryans prevented him from making too much of the incident. Besides, Matthew insisted on going in with her, and explaining that what had happened had been all his fault, and even her grandmother had to concede that Olivia was not to blame.

And, although Olivia thought that that would be the end of the affair, it wasn't. Two days later, her bike was delivered to her, as good as new, and the next weekend

Matthew himself appeared, ostensibly to assure himself that all was well.

He arrived as the family were about to sit down to Sunday lunch, and Olivia's mother invited him to join them. 'It's so seldom we have visitors,' she exclaimed, and Olivia remembered how her mother had looked at her as she made the suggestion. Almost as if she had known that Matthew's reasons for being there had little to do with checking up on Sam Pollack's repair.

Of course, her grandmother didn't approve, but in spite of her illness Felicity Stoner was still mistress in her own home, and Matthew needed no second invitation. He shared their roast beef and Yorkshire pudding with every indication of enjoying it, and afterwards, he helped Olivia wash up, as if doing so was something he did every day of his life.

And it was while they were alone in the kitchen, that he asked her to Rycroft the following weekend. 'I'm having a party,' he said. 'Just a few of the students from college, and one or two people from around here who you'll probably know already.'

Olivia didn't know what to say. She desperately wanted to go, but she suspected her parents would never agree to it. Not unless she could persuade them that Matthew's parents had invited her.

'Doesn't it appeal to you?' Matthew was asking, and she shook her head before dipping her hands back into the soapy water.

'It's not that.'

'Then what is it?'

'Oh——' Olivia lifted her shoulders. 'I don't know if—if my father will let me come. Perhaps, if your mother——'

'My parents are away,' said Matthew flatly. 'They're down in the Caribbean, enjoying the sunshine. That's why I'm having the party this coming weekend. They're due back the following Tuesday.'

'Oh.' Olivia bent her head, her hair, which in those days she wore in a single braid, dipping over one shoulder. 'Well, it's very kind of you to ask me, but——'

'You're not going to turn me down, are you?' Matthew gazed at her appealingly. 'Hey—I only organised this party so I'd have an excuse for seeing you again!'

Olivia's face flamed. 'That's not true!'

'It is true.' Matthew put the tea-towel he had been holding down, and came to stand next to her. 'I want to see you again.' He lifted his hand and brushed a tendril of silky blonde hair back from her forehead. 'Don't you want to see me, too?'

Olivia swallowed. 'I—well—yes.' Her experiences with boys of her own age had hardly prepared her for Matthew's practised approach. 'But—I—my father's very strict.'

'You mean he doesn't trust me?'

'I—not exactly.'

Olivia was on unsure ground here. She had the feeling her father wouldn't like to think she was implying that he didn't trust his landlord's son. But, at the same time, she knew Robert Stoner was unlikely to approve of her attending a party, particularly at Rycroft. And particularly if Matthew's parents weren't there.

Matthew's hand dropped from her temple, his knuckles grazing her cheek in passing. 'OK,' he said, his grey eyes warmly intent. 'So, I'll scrub the idea of a party. Do you think he'd let me take you to the pictures in Abbot's Norton instead?'

Olivia stared at him. 'But why?' she asked impulsively, unable to believe he really did want to take her out, and Matthew pulled a face.

'You're not supposed to ask questions like that,' he remarked, propping his hips against the sink beside her. 'Why do you think? Because I like you, and I want to spend some time with you.'

Olivia shook her head a little disbelievingly. 'But—you know lots of girls.'

Matthew shrugged. 'So?'

'More—suitable—girls,' appended Olivia, trying to concentrate on the saucepan she was scouring, which wasn't easy, with Matthew's thigh brushing hers. 'Like— Helen Berrenger, for example.'

'If you don't want to see me again, just say so,' said Matthew drily. 'There's no need for this elaborate charade. I can take it.'

Olivia turned her head to look at him. He was looking at her, and for a few moments they just stared at one another. And then, very gently, he took hold of her wrist and pulled her towards him, and his mouth brushed hers once, then twice, and then more urgently, as her lips parted.

As a first kiss it was pretty intense, and Matthew was breathing rather heavily when he drew back. 'Does that mean you'll come?' he asked huskily, his thumb stroking across her mouth, and Olivia thought unsteadily that wild horses wouldn't keep her away.

Of course, it wasn't easy to begin with. Although Matthew had gained her father's permission to take Olivia to the cinema on that first occasion, subsequent meetings were harder to arrange. Robert Stoner had not been able to deny Matthew's request when it was made personally, but finding reasons why Olivia couldn't see him again were simpler to contrive.

And in this undertaking he was ably assisted by his mother. Harriet Stoner made her disapproval of the relationship plain, and Olivia's father used this to re-inforce his own opinion that the association should not continue.

'I don't know what Lady Lavinia would say, if she knew,' he declared, when Olivia asked if she could attend a rally-cross meeting with Matthew, on his next free weekend. 'Livvy, people like us don't get involved with people like the Ryans. Young Matthew's just attracted by a pretty face, that's all. And I'm not having you become the talk of the village, getting into trouble of that sort.'

'Of what sort?'

Olivia was indignant, and when her father flushed with embarrassment her grandmother clicked her tongue. 'You know of what sort, Livvy Stoner!' she retorted, her narrow face harsh with impatience. 'You're not a child, for all you act like one sometimes. The likes of Matthew Ryan are not for you. You know it, and he knows it. And mark my words, he's only taking you out because he thinks you're easy game!'

CHAPTER SEVEN

But Olivia didn't believe either of them. Maybe she had been rather naïve in that respect, she admitted now, but events had proved that her trust in Matthew had not been misplaced. Far from keeping their association a secret from his family, Olivia had become a regular visitor at Rycroft, and although she had never felt entirely at home with his mother she had learned to hold her own with the young people the Ryans cultivated.

So far as her relationship with Matthew was concerned, that had quickly accelerated. Although she had worried that the difference in their ages might prove a problem, it hadn't. After all, she had turned seventeen just a few months later, and with the added year had come an added maturity. It had given her the confidence to stand up to both her father and her grandmother, and, looking back on it now, she realised her mother had always been her strongest ally. *Her mother . . .*

Forcing that thought aside, Olivia remembered how Matthew used to take her out in his car, his 'hot' Mini, as he laughingly used to call it. Hot, in more ways than one, she reflected ruefully. When they were together, Matthew had only had to touch her for her blood to turn to liquid fire.

And that had proved a problem, she conceded, recalling the necking sessions they had had in Matthew's car. Until Matthew, her experience of sex had been confined to wet kisses after the village disco, and fighting off any boy who tried to go further. But with Matthew she found she didn't want to fight him off, and what usually began as a casual touching of mouths rapidly turned to a passionate embrace.

She knew Matthew had tried to keep control of the situation. Once, he had even broken off in the middle of a particularly sensuous exchange, and got out of the car and left her. But the truth was, she had been as guilty as Matthew of wanting more than he was giving her, and every time they were together the temptation got stronger and stronger.

One evening in early October, Matthew took her for a meal in Salisbury. It was in the nature of a farewell treat. The following day he was returning to university, and although he had every intention of spending every free weekend at home, for the past three months they had been together every day. Consequently the separation was going to be that much harder, and Olivia was not looking forward to all those empty evenings.

They drove home slowly, parking, as they usually did, overlooking the river, and the weir where they had first exchanged the retriever puppy. Sandy was a working dog now, of course, but he had occasionally accompanied them on outings to Salisbury Plain, or the coast. To-night, of course, he was not with them, but Olivia couldn't help feeling grateful to him for his part in their relationship.

It was late, but it wasn't totally dark. The moon had risen, and the car was illuminated by its silvery light. Sufficiently so for Matthew to see Olivia's wistful expression, and he bent his head to nuzzle her ear with his lips.

'Cheer up,' he said huskily. 'I'll be back in five days.'

'Five days!' said Olivia, sighing, and turning to look at him. Her hand cupped his jaw. 'That sounds like a lifetime.'

'I know.' Matthew turned his mouth against her palm. 'But it will pass, believe me. And at the end of this coming year I'll have my degree.'

'Mmm.' Olivia brushed her thumb across his lower lip, and when his lips parted she rubbed the sensitive inner side. 'And then, I suppose, you'll go and live in London. Didn't you say that's what you wanted to do?'

'I said *we'd* go and live in London,' corrected Matthew, taking hold of her thumb, and biting the pad. 'Why are you being so negative? What has your father been saying now?'

Olivia bent her head. 'What does he usually say?' she asked resignedly. 'You know he doesn't approve of our friendship. I dare say both he and my grandmother will consider your return to college as the end of our relationship. They've already told me that you probably know girls at college who have far more in common with you than I do.'

'Oh, *God*!' Matthew's hand at her nape turned her face up to his. 'Now, you don't believe that, do you?'

Olivia lifted her shoulders. 'No. Yes. I don't know.' She was confused, and unhappy, and Matthew closed his eyes for a moment, against the haunted beauty of hers.

'Don't do this to me, Liv,' he groaned, bringing her head forward, and resting his forehead against hers. 'You know how I feel about you. I've never made any secret of it. I'm not saying I haven't dated girls in London; of course I have. But none of them meant anything to me. And since you and I started going out together—well, there's been no one else, and you know it.'

'Do I?' Olivia looked at him out of the corners of her eyes, the tip of her tongue appearing to moisten her upper lip.

'Yes.' Matthew looked impatient now. 'God, what are you saying? That you don't believe me? I swear to you, I've not dated anyone else since I took you home that afternoon your bike was damaged. And that's the truth.'

Olivia caught her lower lip between her teeth. 'But Gran said——'

She broke off, but Matthew wouldn't let her finish there. 'Go on,' he said harshly. 'What did she say? I know she doesn't like me, so it won't come as any surprise.'

Olivia hesitated. 'It's not important.'

'If it comes between you and me, it is important,' retorted Matthew fervently. He cupped her face between his hands, and brushed her mouth with his. 'Go on. You can tell me. Who am I supposed to have seen?'

Olivia moved her chin out of his hands. 'It wasn't that.'

'Then what was it?'

'I can't say.'

'Can't? Or won't?' enquired Matthew disgustedly. Then, as if realising what was happening, he uttered a coarse oath. 'Can't you see what she's doing to us? She's making us fight with each other!'

'No, she's not.'

But Olivia was scared that he was right, even if she didn't say so. His lean, attractive face was so full of frustration that, abandoning her anxieties, she looped her arms around his neck, and brought his lips to hers. Then, opening her mouth against his, as he had taught her to do, she tentatively sought his tongue with her own.

Matthew didn't respond at first, but when Olivia loosened first her coat and then his leather jacket, and pressed herself against him, his resistance failed. Forcing her back against the seat, he thrust his tongue into her mouth with half-angry aggression. It was as if he needed to prove to himself, as well as to her, that he could still control the situation, but for once his plan backfired. The silky cavern of her mouth, the sensuous brush of her tongue against his, and the budding pressure of her breasts against his chest, were simply too inflammatory in his present mood of desperation. Senses began to spin out of control, and, instead of drawing back when the flame he had ignited began to burn too hotly, Matthew continued to feed it.

He wasn't wholly to blame. Olivia was a more than willing pupil, eager to do anything to silence the doubts her grandmother had planted in her mind. Matthew wanted her, only her; he had been wanting her for the past six months; and if this was what was needed to hold him, she would let him have her.

But that was the last coherent thought she had. It simply wasn't possible to think at all, with Matthew using all his not-inconsiderable skills to arouse her temperature to fever pitch. It wasn't the first time he had put his hand beneath her sweater, and touched her breasts, but tonight he wasn't content with just holding their rounded fullness in his hands. Instead, he dragged the sweater up beneath her arms, and bent his head to take their rosy peaks into his mouth.

Olivia shuddered as he sucked on the swollen nipples. Her knowledge of lovemaking had not prepared her for how she would feel at seeing Matthew's dark head against her pale skin, but the instinctive sensuality of her nature responded to his. The sensations he was creating were causing a strange melting feeling in the pit of her stomach, and she found herself lifting her breasts to him, and clutching his head against her.

His mouth returned to hers, his breathing heavier now, and Olivia found she was breathing heavily, too, dragging the air into her lungs with an obvious effort. But with her arms around Matthew's neck, her fingers tangled in the damp hair at his nape, she was drowning in emotions she had barely known existed. And, although it was chilly in the car, she didn't feel the cold. All she was aware of was Matthew, and when his hand gripped her knee before sliding along the thigh, under the hem of her skirt, she parted her legs automatically.

'Oh, Christ!'

As Matthew's fingers brushed the throbbing junction of her legs, he abruptly withdrew his hand, and threw himself back in his seat. Raking hands that shook a little through the dusky thickness of his hair, he gave Olivia a sidelong glance, and then, meeting her confused eyes, he added, harshly, 'Pull your sweater down.'

'What? Oh!' Olivia was too bewildered to understand what had happened, but she knew that for some reason Matthew was angry with her, and as sanity returned she fumbled her sweater back into place. 'I'm sorry.'

'Don't,' he muttered. 'Don't—be sorry. It's I who should be saying that to you. God, I must be going out of my mind!'

'Why?' Olivia swallowed. 'Because you wanted me?'

Matthew slumped down in his seat, turning his head against the back-rest until he was looking at her. 'Don't be stupid!' he said impatiently, and then, seeing her instinctive look of injury, he shook his head. 'No,' he declared, 'you're not stupid, I am.'

'Why?' Olivia forced herself to meet his frustrated gaze, and after a moment's hesitation Matthew leaned across and took her hand, and brought it to the hard ridge that swelled against his flat stomach. 'Oh!'

'Yes. Oh,' agreed Matthew, closing his eyes against the exquisite sensation of her soft fingers probing his arousal. 'You know what you do to me.'

Olivia licked her lips. Just occasionally, when they had been dancing together, or when Matthew said goodnight, she had felt a little of the effect she had on him, but he had always kept it well under control. This was different. This was serious. And this was what her grandmother had meant!

'Does—does it hurt?' she asked, and flushed at the realisation of how naïve she must sound. But Matthew's lips only twitched with a faintly self-derisory amusement.

'You could say that,' he agreed at last, pushing himself up in the seat, and replacing her hand in her lap. 'We'd better go.'

'No—wait.' Olivia bit the inner flesh of her lower lip. 'What—what will you do?'

'Do?' Matthew frowned. 'Take you home, of course. What else?'

'No—I mean—what will you do about—about that.' She flicked a nervous hand towards his lower abdomen.

Matthew stilled in his attempt to start the engine. 'Say that again?' he said, uncomprehendingly, and Olivia heaved an unhappy sigh.

'Do you—I mean—after we—after we've been together, do you—go—with someone else?' she asked,
almost inaudibly. 'I—I'd like to know.'

'Would you?'

Matthew's lean face had hardened considerably, and
Olivia was very much afraid she had overstepped the
bounds of their relationship. In consequence, she hurried
on, rather rashly, 'I mean—men do, don't they? If—if
they don't get satisfaction in one place, they look for it
in—in another.'

Matthew's expression was not encouraging. 'Who told
you that?' he demanded harshly. 'Oh, don't tell me. I
can guess. It was your grandmother, wasn't it?' He stared
at her accusingly. 'That was what you were trying to say
earlier. She's spun you some tale about a man always
wanting sex!'

Olivia shivered. 'Isn't it true?'

Matthew's hands clenched on the wheel. 'Maybe.'

Olivia's eyes widened. 'Do you mean you have been
with some other girl after——?'

'No. Christ, *no*!' Matthew swore bitterly. 'Liv, I'm a
man, not an animal! Oh, I'm not denying I want you.
God, you know that! And if I was to say it's always easy
that wouldn't be true. But I'm not cheating on you either.
I care about you too much for that.'

Olivia shook her head. 'Then—then why don't
we——?'

'What?' Matthew's lips tightened. 'Have it off in the
back of the car?' His voice was rough. 'Is that what you
want?'

Olivia quivered. 'Don't say it like that. It sounds—it
sounds——'

'Crude?' he enquired grimly. 'Well, it would be,
wouldn't it? Exactly what your grandmother expects of
me, I dare say. Only I'm not going to oblige her.'

Olivia hesitated. 'But—we can't go on like this, can
we?'

'We have to,' said Matthew, starting the car.

'So—when—when will we——?'

'When we're married, I guess,' he replied, startling
her into silence. 'Now, can we talk about something else?
There are limits to what even I can stand.'

Of course, they hadn't waited until they were married,
Olivia remembered achingly. Soon after Matthew went
back to college she had given up studying for her A levels,
and found herself a job. It had caused friction in the
family, naturally, but it was the only way she could think
of to be at least partly independent.

Nevertheless, there had been a lot of hard words
spoken when it was revealed that Olivia had got a job
in Winchester so that she could catch the late afternoon
train to London. The job she had found, as an assistant
nanny with a playgroup, freed her at five o'clock, and
she could be in London, with Matthew, by a quarter to
seven.

Coming back however, was a little more difficult. The
latest she could leave London was a quarter to ten, if
she wanted to catch a connecting bus to Lower Mychett.
And, after the rather hairy experience of missing her
connection one evening and having to take a taxi, she
began to spend the homeward journey on the edge of
her seat.

When Matthew found out what had happened, he was
tight-lipped for days. Anything could have happened to
her, he said. A young girl, travelling alone with a man
at that time of night. A week later, although he had seen
her off at Waterloo as usual, he was waiting when Olivia
reached the other end.

'I'll come down to Winchester from now on,' he said,
as the little Mini skidded down the icy track to the farm.
'I can always spend the night at Rycroft, and drive back
to town in the morning. I'd never forgive myself if anything happened to you. You mean too much to me.'

Of course, Olivia argued with him that it simply wasn't
sensible for him to drive all the way from London, and
then drive back again. She said that she had got a job
so that she could come to meet him, not vice versa. Besides, she added, he needed a good night's rest, to con-

centrate on getting his degree. If he was going to spend
his time driving up and down to Hampshire, his work
was bound to suffer.

They argued all the way to the farm, and even after
they got there the subject was not resolved. It was only
when Olivia threatened not to see him through the week
that Matthew submitted. And even then he made her
promise to ring her father and have him drive into
Winchester and pick her up if she ever missed her bus
again.

Olivia agreed, although she knew her father would be
unlikely to make the journey more than once. So far,
she had managed to convince him that she could look
after herself. He knew nothing about her missing the
bus, or having to take a taxi. However, if she ever had
to call on him for assistance, the truth was bound to
come out. And although he couldn't actually forbid her
to see Matthew, he could make life impossible at home.

As it was, it wasn't brilliant. Her relationship with
Matthew was frowned on by everyone but her mother.
Even her best friend, Jenny Mason, thought she was
crazy to take him seriously. Everyone was waiting for
her to prove she had made a fool of herself. How, she
wasn't sure, unless they expected Matthew to drop her.

Anyway, Olivia refused to let anything come between
them, and a couple of weeks later she caught the usual
train to London. However, when she got to Waterloo,
Matthew wasn't there. For the first time since she had
started making this journey he wasn't waiting on the
platform, and she wondered with a sinking heart if he
had got tired of her at last.

But surely he would have told her? Surely he wouldn't
have allowed her to make this journey for nothing? And
how was she supposed to find out? She didn't even know
his telephone number.

She thought about ringing Rycroft, just in case he was
there, but she quickly discarded the idea. She didn't even
know if Matthew's parents knew what she was doing.
And what could she say if they said he was at home?

Standing about on Waterloo Station was not sensible,
however. She was already receiving some rather disturbing stares from the kind of men who hung about
such places. The last thing she wanted was for them to
think she had run away from home, and needed their
assistance. When Matthew had come to meet her, they
had usually gone for a meal somewhere; or to a bar,
where no one noticed what they were doing. Food had
always been of secondary importance to just being alone
together, and they had kissed a lot, and held hands,
without the pressures that being alone could bring.

But perhaps Matthew had got tired of just playing
around. Perhaps the teasing delight she had gained from
running her hand along his thigh had begun to pall.
Perhaps he had wanted more than that tantalising ex-
ploration, but because of her father's involvement he
had decided to find someone else.

And then a hand touched her sleeve, and she swung
round in alarm to find a young man of about Matthew's
age right behind her. 'Excuse me——' he began, smiling,
but before he could get any further, Olivia jerked away
from him.

'Leave me alone!' she exclaimed in alarm, glancing
round to see if he had an accomplice. 'If you don't go
away, I'll call a policeman——'

'Hold on.' The young man raised a soothing hand.
'It's OK. Matt sent me. Matt Ryan, right? You are
Olivia—Liv, aren't you? He said I should look for the
most beautiful girl around.'

Olivia gulped, her panic subsiding. 'You know—
Matthew?'

'I should do. We've been living next door to one
another for the past two years. I'm Cormac—*Mac*—
Connolly. But I don't suppose he's mentioned me.'

'Mac?' Olivia was weak with relief. 'Oh—oh, yes. Yes,
he has mentioned you.' She swallowed convulsively, and
then another thought struck her. 'But—what are you
doing here? Where's Matt?' Her heart skipped a beat.
'Is something wrong?'

'You could say that.' Mac was laconic, and then seeing her anxious expression, he grinned. 'Hey, it's nothing serious. Matt's cracked a bone in his ankle, that's all. But he's got to wear a cast for the next six weeks.'

Olivia was dismayed, and not just because of Matthew's injury, although that was worrying enough. But also because of what it would mean to them. If Matthew was confined to the university, he wouldn't be able to see her. Or come home at weekends, if he couldn't drive his car.

Now, she managed to shake her head and say politely, 'What a shame. Poor Matt. Um—how did he do it?'

'He was playing rugby,' said Mac cheerfully. 'We occasionally get a team together, and play the local club. We were both free this afternoon, so we volunteered. But Matt got kicked as he was making a try, and although he didn't want to go and get it X-rayed the club coach insisted.' He grimaced. 'It was just as well he did. He was in a lot of pain.'

'And now?' asked Olivia tensely. 'Is he all right now?'

'Well, they've pumped him full of pain-killers, but he's OK. Anyway, you'll see for yourself. Shall we go?'

'Go?' Olivia stared at him in confusion.

'Sure. You're coming to see him, aren't you?' Mac grimaced. 'You'd better. I've got strict orders to bring you straight back to Hall.'

'Hall?'

'Halls of Residence,' explained Mac quickly. 'It's just a glorified hostel, really. We each have our own room, of course, but we share the bathrooms, and there's a self-service restaurant of sorts.'

'I see.' Olivia had heard about Matthew's room before, but not in such detail. 'Well—all right.'

'Great. Let's go.'

The rather austere-looking building where Matthew lived while he was at college was situated in a cul-de-sac off Euston Road. Mac took her there in Matthew's car, having been allowed to drive it only because he was picking Olivia up. This he told her in a rather lugubrious tone, but Olivia could tell that he and Matthew were good friends.

However, it was not so reassuring to find out that the building accommodated women as well as men, and as she and Mac went up in the lift several of the girls asked him if Matthew was all right. Evidently news of his accident had spread throughout the college, and although it was good to know that Matthew was so popular Olivia couldn't deny a feeling of jealousy at the ease of access these women had to him.

Matthew's room was on the fourth floor, and Mac breezed in without knocking. 'Here we are,' he said jauntily. 'All present and correct, *sir*!'

Olivia followed, rather less confidently, but when she saw Matthew sitting at the desk beneath the window, his foot, in its plaster cast, propped on a pile of books, her doubts fled. 'Oh, Matt,' she breathed, rushing across the room to hug him, and as Matthew pulled her down on to his knees Mac made a tactical retreat.

'Sorry about this,' Matthew said huskily, when he was able to get his breath. 'I should have had more sense. Particularly in the circumstances.'

'What circumstances?' Olivia smoothed the silky dark hair back from his forehead, and Matthew sighed.

'Me coming up and down to Rycroft,' he said ruefully. 'I'm not going to be able to drive the car for the next six weeks.'

'Oh, I see.' Olivia glanced down. 'I'm not too heavy, am I?'

'No.' Matthew's hand slid possessively under her hair, and drew her mouth down to his again. 'I guess I'll have to use the train, but we'll have nowhere to meet, other than pubs or eating places, will we?'

Olivia hesitated. 'You could come to the farm?'

'And face your father's eagle eye? Oh, yes, I could do that.' Matthew grimaced. 'Or you could come to Rycroft, but we both know how little privacy we'd have there.'

Olivia stroked his cheek. 'I'll just have to come up to town at weekends,' she ventured softly. 'If you could find me somewhere to stay.'

'You could stay here,' said Matthew at once, his expression brightening. 'Oh—not in this room,' he amended, as a faint flush of colour stained her cheeks. 'Although I wouldn't object,' he added. 'But no. There are guest rooms on every floor. Rather grand affairs, actually, with their own bathroom!' He grinned. 'I could get you one of them, easily.'

Olivia's eyes brightened. 'All right.'

'But—what will you tell your parents?'

Olivia frowned. 'The truth, I think. Why not? We're not doing anything wrong.'

Of course, Mr Stoner did not approve of the arrangement, but once again it was Olivia's mother who eased the situation. 'You can't expect Olivia not to see Matthew for the next six weeks,' she exclaimed, when the problem was explained to her. 'Good heavens, Bob, she's almost eighteen. She knows what she's doing, and I'd rather she was with Matthew than with someone we don't know.'

As it happened, Olivia's grandmother was away at the time, or she guessed they would not have overcome her father's opposition so easily. As it was, he bowed to his wife's decision, and by the time Harriet Stoner came back the arrangements were made.

And, from Olivia's point of view, it was all quite new and exciting. Until then, her knowledge of London had been limited to a school trip when she was thirteen, and the little she had learned since meeting Matthew. But now she got to know the city very well, and without the petty restrictions of Lower Mychett she lost much of her earlier shyness.

But sleeping in the same building as Matthew was not as easy as she had imagined it would be. For one thing, it got harder and harder to let him go in the evenings, and he refused to let her come to his room after nine o'clock at night, because she never wanted to leave. Instead, he came to her room, and left when the situation became untenable.

And then, inevitably, one evening he didn't leave...

CHAPTER EIGHT

THEY had spent the evening at a disco, Olivia remembered now, held in the common-room downstairs, and Matthew had been forced to spend his time watching her dancing with one after another of his fellow students. He hadn't wanted to go to the disco in the first place, but for once Mac had interfered, and told him that Olivia deserved some fun.

'You can't expect her to sit in every evening, holding your hand,' he told his friend reprovingly. 'Hell, *you* wouldn't like it, would you?'

'OK. We'll go,' Matthew retorted, with an edge to his voice, and Mac had winked at Olivia as he left them.

Of course, Olivia said she didn't really want to go either, but Matthew decided, somewhat tersely, that Mac was right. 'I don't suppose it is much fun for you, spending Saturday nights watching television,' he declared, pushing himself up from his chair. He lent her his portable television at weekends, and they generally watched it together. 'I'll go and get changed,' he added. 'I'll knock on your door in about an hour.'

Olivia had to agree, even though sitting watching television with Matthew was just as enjoyable for her as it was for him, in his present state of disability. So long as they were alone together, she was content, and the idea of spending the evening with a lot of other people wasn't all that appealing.

Still, Matthew had made up his mind, and to please him she changed into a new pair of jeans, and a round-necked cream sweater. With the gold chain Matthew had bought her for her seventeenth birthday around her neck, she knew she looked good, and she hoped she wouldn't let him down in front of his friends.

But, in the event, she proved to be too popular, and once Mac had convinced everyone that Matthew wasn't going to be selfish she danced every dance. Not that Matthew was neglected. A steady stream of girls shared his corner of the common-room, but when the disco was over they were both distinctly cool with one another.

As usual, Matthew escorted her to the guest-room, but when Olivia asked him if he wanted to come in he shook his head. 'I'm sure you're too tired,' he replied tersely, his grey eyes chilling in their detachment, and Olivia's temper flared.

'Don't you mean you are?' she retorted, tossing her head, and the single plait in which she had confined her hair spilled its ribbon on to the floor.

'What's that supposed to mean?' Matthew bent to pick up the ribbon with an effort, and, watching his struggle to rescue the piece of blue satin, Olivia's anger dissipated.

'Nothing,' she said huskily, and, acting purely on impulse, she ran her hand over the muscled curve of his buttocks.

'Christ, Liv!' Matthew straightened from his stooped position red-faced, and then, meeting her appealing gaze, his eyes darkened. 'What are you trying to do to me?'

Olivia shook her head. 'I know what you do to me,' she answered, taking his hand and drawing him into the room. She closed the door behind him, and dropped the latch. 'Oh, come here, you big baby! Do you honestly think I enjoyed dancing with all those other men tonight?'

'You looked as if you did,' said Matthew unevenly, his mouth rubbing sensuously against hers.

'And what about you?' Olivia protested. 'You weren't feeling any pain, judging by the amount of attention you were attracting!'

'Jealous?'

'Hmm.' Olivia wound her arms around his neck. 'Wouldn't you be?'

'Well, it's not necessary,' he assured her thickly, his hand invading the neckline of her sweater. 'I don't want anyone else.'

'Nor do I,' murmured Olivia, bringing down one hand and loosening the buttons that held the knitted sides of the sweater together. Her tongue circled her lips. 'Let me take this off.'

'No.' Matthew shook his head. 'I don't think that would be a good idea.'

'Well, I do.'

'Well, I don't,' said Matthew, more harshly, releasing her, and moving awkwardly away. 'Do we have anything to drink in here? Like Coke, for example?'

Although he still had the plaster on his ankle, Matthew could walk without crutches now, and in a week or so the plaster would be coming off. Just in time for Christmas, he had said, with some relief, but now Olivia was not so sure. She had got to like spending her weekends in London. Once he was able to drive himself again, he'd come down to Hampshire, and spend his nights at Rycroft.

Now she shrugged, and said she didn't have any Coke. 'You'll just have to get one of your *slaves* to get you some from the machine downstairs,' she declared, playing with the two buttons of her sweater she had unfastened. 'I'm going to bed. As you said, I *am* tired.'

Matthew sighed. 'Liv——'

'What?'

She turned to face him, her hands on her hips, her expression unforgiving, and Matthew gazed at her despairingly. 'You're not the only one who has feelings, you know,' he muttered, grasping her elbows and propelling her now resisting body towards him. 'And stop pretending you don't know the way I feel about you. I've told you often enough, God knows! What do I have to do to prove it? Pin a notice on my chest, or what?'

Olivia's resistance dissolved. 'You could—make love to me,' she whispered, her fingers sliding along the lapels of his sports jacket, and with a groan of submission Matthew hauled her into his arms.

His mouth on hers was savage and unrestrained, and very briefly Olivia was afraid of what she had un-leashed. But then the hungry pressure of his lips, and the wet invasion of his tongue, sent her own senses spinning. It was what she had wanted, after all. Matthew uncontrolled, and at the mercy of his senses.

Her hands slid beneath his jacket, sliding it from his shoulders, and it fell unheeded to the floor. His shirt soon followed, and for the first time she spread her palms against his chest. She found his small nipples with her tongue, and exulted in the power she had over his body. There was something infinitely satisfying in feeling her breasts against his hair-coarsened flesh, and she traced the line of body hair that ran down below his belt.

But when her hands went to his belt, to unfasten the buckle, Matthew's hand stilled hers. 'I'll do it,' he said, looking down at the plaster cast with some impatience. 'This—this takes a bit of time. And—well, Mac usually helps me with it.'

'I'll help you,' said Olivia huskily, urging him back towards the bed. 'Go on. Let me. I like the idea of taking your clothes off.'

Matthew's breathing was uneven. 'Liv——' he pro-tested, but when the backs of his knees bumped into the bed he lost his balance, and sat down rather unex-pectedly. And Olivia took the opportunity to kneel down beside him, and urge him back against the cushions, finding his mouth with hers, as her hand probed the belt. But she was not unaware of the hard pressure that swelled against his zipper, or her own lack of experience when she'd succeeded in removing his clothes.

But for the moment she preferred not to look as she loosened the buckle, and unzipped his jeans. She wasn't at all sure if he was wearing anything under his jeans, and she preferred to feel, rather than look. It was im-mature, she knew, but she'd never seen a man naked before. And while the prospect might sound exciting, it was also rather daunting.

However, beneath the jeans, her hands brushed against silk, and she realised he was wearing underpants. Thank goodness, she thought, having confidence enough now to ease the jeans down over his hips. Though she still averted her eyes from the rampant signs of his masculinity, and a tremor of uncertainty slid along her spine.

In fact, the jeans came off more easily than she had expected. They had been slit around the ankle, to allow access for the cast, and it was a simple matter to pull off the one boot he was wearing, and peel the jeans down his legs. Or perhaps, it just seemed easier than she had expected, she thought. Perhaps she was already regretting the impulse to take control.

But, as if guessing how she was feeling, Matthew sat up as she was lingering over folding his jeans and placing them neatly on the floor beside the bed. 'Come here,' he said, lifting her up on to the quilt beside him, and rolling over so that his weight was now imprisoning her to the bed. 'I didn't realise you were so experienced,' he added huskily, burying his head between her breasts, and she shuddered beneath him.

'I'm not,' she confessed, and she felt his teeth brush her skin as he uttered a soft laugh.

'I'd never have guessed,' he said teasingly, but then his humour disappeared as his mouth found hers again.

Her breasts were crushed against his chest, and his leg eased its way between hers. It made it easier for him to cup the swelling mound of her womanhood, and she twisted against him as he touched her there. But her clothes were still an intolerable barrier, and, sensing the needs she herself hardly understood, Matthew's hand moved to the button of her jeans.

'Help me,' he breathed, against her lips, and she obediently lifted her hips, so that he could ease the denim down over her hips.

Now, only the scrap of cotton and lace that formed her underwear was between her and his eyes, and Olivia trembled. Matthew was looking at her with a frankly sensual expression in his eyes, and although she wanted to be cool and sophisticated she didn't know how.

Then, he bent his head and trailed a line of kisses from the curve of her breast, across her flat abdomen, to the dusky hollow of her navel. His lips were on a level with the ribbon-trimmed elastic of the panties now, but when he would have brushed them aside Olivia stopped him.

'No, Matthew,' she said, clutching a handful of his hair, and he looked up at her through lazy-lidded eyes.

'Why not?' he asked, taking the elastic between his teeth, and tugging very gently. 'You're beautiful, and I want to see you. All of you. You're not going to stop me now, are you?'

Olivia breathed unevenly. 'I—well, could we turn out the light first?' she ventured, indicating the lamp on the table beside the bed, but Matthew only pulled a wry face.

'I said I wanted to see you,' he reminded her softly, his thumbs hooking into the ribbon-trimmed band, and easing them down, until his lips brushed the cluster of gold curls that sprang out from their confinement. 'Mmm, you are delicious,' he told her, as she felt herself weaken. 'Come on, baby. I'll let you do the same for me.'

Olivia swallowed. The muscles on the insides of her thighs were quivering, but in spite of her fears she wanted to do what he said. 'I—all right,' she said huskily, arching up so that he could remove the offending item. Then, as he buried his face between her thighs, she uttered a protesting cry. 'Matthew—you shouldn't!'

'Why shouldn't I?' he asked, lifting his head and looking at her. 'I love you, and I want to make love with you. But I want you to want me, too.'

Olivia licked her lips. 'I—do,' she protested, and with a half-regretful sigh Matthew moved over her again.

'OK,' he said, drawing her hands to his body. 'But I'm rather over-dressed. Do you want to help me?'

Olivia's lips parted apprehensively, but she didn't draw away when he tucked her fingers into the waistband of

his trunks. With grim determination, she peeled them
down over his taut buttocks, and gasped when his taut
manhood thrust into her hands.

Matthew shuddered then, and, kicking off the trunks,
he lowered his lips to hers. His tongue plunged between
her teeth, hungry and aggressive, and as his tongue rav-
ished her mouth she felt the velvet heat of his desire
nudging the moist junction between her legs. It felt so
big and powerful, throbbing, it seemed, with a life of
its own. It didn't seem possible that she could absorb
him, and her muscles tensed automatically when he
pressed against her.

'Relax,' he breathed against her mouth, his hand
taking the place of his manhood, and creating a trembling awareness of its own. 'You are ready for me, love.
I can feel it. Just let me show you how it can be.'

She rose up against his probing fingers, her legs
splaying helplessly as he brought her to a thrilling
awareness of what he wanted from her. Waves of sensation, that came up from her thighs and swept through
every nerve in her body, caused her to clutch his
shoulders, and beg him to continue. Her breathing
became choked and shallow, and she was no longer conscious of anything but the demanding needs he was
arousing. She arched towards a fulfilment she had not
even known existed, and when it came her senses splin-
tered into a million shattering pieces.

And then, as the blinding tide of pleasure ebbed,
Matthew gently but firmly thrust himself inside her, and
she caught her breath in dismay as a short sharp pain
tore up into her stomach. The delight she had been
feeling, the lazy sense of lethargy that had followed his
manipulation of her body, was replaced by an aching
discomfort, and tears of resentment filled her eyes.

However, Matthew was beyond the point when he
could consider her feelings before his own. His own needs
had taken precedence at last, and although she bucked
against him, he had to find his own release. Shaking his
head, he withdrew part-way, only to thrust once, twice,

against her, and then withdrew completely, shuddering to his own climax outside her body.

For a few moments, Olivia was too shocked to do anything. It had all been so different from what she had expected, and Matthew's withdrawal had been the final humiliation. So much fuss over so little, she thought, edging to the side of the bed. Matthew was still lying with his face hidden within the curve of his arm, and she hoped she could reach her clothes before he realised what she was doing.

But, as she inched away, he grabbed her. 'Don't go, for goodness' sake,' he muttered, forcing himself up on to one elbow and looking down at her. 'I'm sorry about that, but I waited too long, and I couldn't wait any longer.'

Olivia sniffed. 'It doesn't matter——'

'It does matter.' Matthew smoothed a damp tendril of hair back from her forehead. During their love-making, her hair had come loose from its braid, and now it tumbled about her shoulders, soft and appealing. 'I wanted to make it as good for you as it was for me, but—well, I guess I blew it.'

'It doesn't matter,' said Olivia again, turning her head away. 'I—um—oughtn't you to be going? It's getting late.'

Matthew sighed. 'Do you want me to go?'

'Do I——?' Olivia turned back to look at him. 'What do you mean?'

'I mean—I'd like to stay,' said Matthew huskily. 'Oh, Liv, don't look at me like that. I promise I'll make it good for you. At least, give me the chance to try.'

Olivia stared at him. 'W—when?'

Matthew's mouth twisted. 'Now?'

'Now?' Olivia was shocked again. She looked down his body, and then coloured appealingly. 'But—I thought——'

'Yes? What did you think?' Matthew arched a dark eyebrow.

Olivia shook her head. 'I just thought—I mean—*can you*?'

'Mmm.' Matthew brushed her shoulder with his lips. 'If you'll let me.'

Olivia hesitated. 'Will—will you—do what you did before?'

Matthew grimaced. 'I hope not.'

Olivia bit her lip. 'I meant——'

'I know what you meant,' he told her huskily. He caressed the tip of her breast with his tongue. 'And this time, you won't be disappointed.'

Nevertheless, she was apprehensive when Matthew moved between her thighs, but this time when he eased his way into her there was no pain. Just an incredible feeling of fullness, that made her draw up her knees so that he could bury himself inside her.

Matthew was patient this time, letting her body set the pace, and building on her increasing awareness of her own needs. Amazingly, she felt her muscles responding when he began to move, contracting and expanding around him, enclosing him within her silken sheath, until Matthew caught his breath at the pleasure she was giving him.

'You are incredible,' he told her unsteadily, his thumbs finding the hard peaks of her breasts as they surged against his hands. Dipping his head, he laved the taut areola with his tongue, and the sensations he created only added to the excitement he was arousing within her.

But gradually, his pace quickened. The responsive pressure of her body was driving him to thrust himself deeper and deeper into that tight honeycomb, and the desire he was initiating was like a throbbing pulse inside her. It wasn't like before, when he had brought her trembling limbs to that initial climax. This time, she was beginning to think she would go mad with need of him when the convulsive shudders engulfed her. She held on to him, as the waves of pleasure shook her to the core, and when Matthew would have withdrawn again she wrapped her legs about him. Trapped within the silken

curve of her thighs, he jerked uncontrollably against her.
And then, the flooding heat of his seed spurted inside
her, and, unable to prevent the inevitable, he slumped
across her.

And now, Olivia felt no desire to leave him, or to have
him leave her. On the contrary, she felt extraordinarily
content; weak and lethargic, but totally fulfilled. They
had made love, she thought, amazed at her own lack of
inhibition. She had him—all of him—and she would
never let him go.

Of course, Matthew was less enthusiastic when he
eventually dragged himself away from her. 'That was
crazy,' he said, his meaning unmistakable. 'You could
get pregnant!' He grimaced. 'And then what would your
father say?'

'I don't care.' Olivia was totally unrepentant. 'I'd like
to have your baby. I'd like to have lots of babies,' she
told him softly, 'if that's the way we go about it.'

Matthew had to laugh at that, but afterwards he insisted that they took precautions. 'I want you to have
my children, too,' he said. 'But not yet. Not until I finish
university, and can get a job. I want to marry you in the
church at Lower Mychett, in view of everyone. I don't
want us to *have* to get married. I want you to myself,
at least for a while.'

Which had been just as well, thought Olivia now, shaking
her head. What a mess that would have been! If she had
found she was expecting Matthew's baby! She wondered
what her mother would have done then . . .

Of course, she and Matthew had spent every moment
they could together from then on. For the next six
months, they had devised a hundred ways of being alone
together, once even spending a weekend in the Cotswolds,
staying in a thatched-roofed cottage they had leased
through an agency. There had been a tantalising delight
in pretending they were married, in sleeping together in
the big old four-poster bed, and sharing their breakfast
in the sunlit parlour. Olivia had known she had never

been so happy in her life before—or since—and it had
seemed impossible that anyone could take it all away
from her.

But, in June, it had happened. On her eighteenth
birthday, to be precise, she remembered—though why
her grandmother had chosen that occasion to break the
news to her, Olivia could only imagine.

Perhaps, for a while, the old lady had hoped nothing
would come of their relationship. It was an unlikely alliance, after all: the squire's son and the tenant's
daughter; she might have believed that Matthew's father
would not allow their association to continue. Or her
daughter-in-law...

That jealousy might have played some part in her
grandmother's scheme of things, Olivia had tried not to
believe. In spite of everything, she was the woman who
had brought her up, who had, in many ways, taken her
mother's place. Could she have hated her so much?
Olivia could only speculate. Whatever, she had maintained that as a Christian—as a loyal member of the
church—she could not, in all conscience, allow this
abomination to continue. And Olivia had been in no
state to deny her.

Nevertheless, she had chosen to reveal the information she possessed on the most important evening of
Olivia's young life. The evening when she came of age,
and Matthew's parents were throwing a party in her
honour. Matthew had said it was their way of announcing to the district in general, and to the Stoners
in particular, that they approved of their son's relationship with her, and Olivia's mother had even cajoled
Robert Stoner into wearing a dinner-jacket for the
occasion.

Looking back on it now, Olivia recalled her own
feelings as she accompanied her parents to Rycroft. There
had been anticipation, certainly, but not any pleasurable
intent. Indeed, she had tried to get out of going, but of
course that had been impossible. Instead she had gone
with them, feeling as if someone had drained every drop

of blood from her body; as if the waxy pallor of her face was in some way indicative of the fact that the girl she had been that morning had died and been replaced by a zombie.

And all because her grandmother had come into her bedroom as she was getting ready for the party, and told her that Matthew was her brother... Well, half-brother, really, Olivia amended now, her eyes flickering irresistibly over his lean dark face. The stories she had never really believed, that Matthew's father had been something of a philanderer in his youth, were true. He really had sown his wild oats, both before and after his marriage to Lady Lavinia. He and Felicity Stoner—or Felicity Jennings, as she had been then—had had an affair. And she, Olivia, was the result of that unhappy alliance. Robert Stoner wasn't her father at all. Matthew's father was.

Naturally, she hadn't believed it. Hadn't wanted to believe it, anyway. Even though it had explained her grandmother's attitude towards her over the years. Besides, she argued, her mother would have told her. She, of all people, must know how she and Matthew felt about one another.

But here her grandmother destroyed what little hope she had left. No one knew, she said. Matthew's father didn't know. So far as he, and everyone else was concerned, Olivia was Robert Stoner's child. Even the man she called her father believed that she was his daughter. How could Felicity have told her, when it would mean the destruction of her own marriage?

For a while, Olivia had felt numb, incapable of thought, and certainly incapable of reason. The magnitude of what her grandmother had told her was such that for a few minutes she couldn't even remember what she was doing.

But then the pain had come, sweeping down on her like the sword of Damocles, that had been hanging over her, unknowingly, all these years. And with the pain had come the need to deny what she had heard, to refute the things her grandmother was saying, and argue that, if it had been such a closely guarded secret, how could anyone prove that it was true?

And that was when Harriet Stoner had produced the letters, the letters Matthew's father had written to her mother, and which had proved, beyond a shadow of a doubt, that they had been having an affair. She hadn't wanted to read them. They were private, she'd said. But her grandmother had made her, standing over her as she did so, pointing out the relevant phrases that revealed the intimacy of their relationship.

How her grandmother had got hold of those letters, Olivia had never found out. It had been sufficient to know that they were still around, that Felicity had felt incapable of destroying them, even after all these years. Had she kept them because she had intended telling her daughter one day? Or were they simply a memento, a reminder of the recklessness of youth?

But it was one of Felicity's own letters that betrayed her guilt.

> My darling Matt,
> I am going to have a baby; our baby. I'm telling you, because I know it's what you've always wanted, and I wanted to share it with you. But I know you have Lavinia to think about, and it's not going to be easy, for either of us. Indeed, sometimes I think it would be better if we never saw one another again. Bob loves me. I know that. And I love him. But I'll never love anyone as I love you. Believe that. Fliss.

'But—how do you know that——?' Olivia had begun desperately, as she put the hateful letter aside, and in answer her grandmother had produced two certificates. One was her parents' marriage certificate, the date, in December, only now acquiring some significance. The other, as if she had needed to see it, was her own birth certificate, dated some seven months later.

'But if—if you knew my mother was expecting another man's child when she married my—father,' Olivia had stumbled, 'why didn't you tell him?'

'Because I didn't know,' her grandmother had replied quellingly. 'Your mother didn't leave these letters lying around, you know. It was only after you were born that I became suspicious.'

Olivia had shaken her head. 'I don't understand——'

'Your mother and my son were childhood sweethearts,' the old lady had declared coldly. 'It was always expected that one day they'd get married, and that was how it was. Matthew Ryan—the older Matthew Ryan, I mean—was probably just an aberration. She never loved him. Oh, I know what she says in her letter, but the facts don't bear this out. Felicity loved my son. She had always loved my son. She was just—flattered by Matt Ryan's attentions. And that man took advantage of it.'

Of course, she had asked more questions, desperately trying to find some loophole in her grandmother's story; but there was none. When she asked why her grandmother hadn't confronted her mother with the evidence, Mrs Stoner had been quite pragmatic. What would have been the point? she said. They were already married, *happily* married. So far as her son was concerned, he had a new baby daughter. Why should she destroy his happiness for the sake of a bastard child?

Olivia had been sick then, violently sick. She had locked herself in the bathroom, and wished she had the courage to use her father's razor on her wrists. Life had lost all meaning. She no longer wanted to go on living. If the man she loved was forbidden to her, what earthly use was there in going on?

Looking back now, Olivia realised how melodramatic she had been. Hearts didn't break; they only cracked a little. But at eighteen, she had been young, and desperately in love. Desperate enough to see no future, just the wreckage of the past.

But, somehow, they had persuaded her that she had to go to the party. Of course, her parents hadn't known what had turned the light-hearted girl who had wakened up that morning into the pale ghost they accompanied to Rycroft, but they had been determined that she shouldn't let them down. They probably thought she and Matthew had had a row, she reflected, and, sure enough, before the party was over, that was what had happened. Matthew had been much less tolerant of her reasons for appearing like a skeleton at the feast. His sympathies had been decidedly strained, and when he had produced an engagement ring and she had turned him down, the angry words had come, thick and fast.

However, Olivia had found that anger had given her the strength to get through the rest of that dreadful evening. Even though she had had to contend with her father's contempt, too, on the way home. Robert Stoner had been blind to everything but the fact that, somehow, his daughter had shamed him, and without the right to reveal the truth Olivia hadn't said a word in her own defence.

But it must have been harder still for her mother, Olivia reflected now. Had she guessed what had happened? In the days that had followed, when Olivia went around silent and uncommunicative, had she suspected anything? There was no way of knowing, even now. It was a subject that had always, and must always, remain taboo. And Olivia had had too hard a time keeping Matthew at bay to feel much sympathy for anyone else.

CHAPTER NINE

THE day of the funeral proved to be just as hot as the day before. Olivia could feel the sun beating down on the shoulders of her navy silk suit, as she stood beside the open grave in the churchyard. She felt sorry for her sister, wilting beside her. In these latter stages of her pregnancy, Sara was feeling the heat, and Olivia guessed she missed the support of her absent husband.

Across the grave, Olivia saw that the Ryans had turned out in force. Matthew's father—*her father?*—was there, and Lady Lavinia. And Matthew himself, of course, dark and disturbing in his charcoal-grey suit. Would she ever look at Matthew objectively? she wondered. Even now, knowing what she did, he still made her senses burn.

Surprisingly, Helen wasn't with him. Or perhaps not so surprisingly, she thought, trying to think impartially. After all, she doubted Helen even knew of her grandmother's existence. And just because she was married to Matthew was no reason to share all his responsibilities.

She allowed her gaze to move to Matthew's father, trying to be impartial about him, too. And, whatever way she looked at it, she couldn't feel that he had any connection with her life. He might be her natural parent, but Robert Stoner was her father.

She had wondered how she would feel, seeing him again, but she felt nothing. She wondered how he felt, looking across the grave at the woman who had once been his mistress. Did he feel anything? Did her mother feel anything? Or had it been, as her grandmother had said, just a fleeting aberration?

The vicar's words came to an end, and the silence in the graveyard was broken only by the patter of soil falling on the coffin. Robert Stoner had stooped to make his

110

final farewell to his mother, and Olivia turned aside, ashamed of feeling so little.

And it was then that she saw the look that passed between her mother and Matthew's father. She doubted anyone else noticed. Like all good Christian men and women, most were intent on paying their last respects to the deceased—or appearing to do so, which, in a place like Lower Mychett, was equally important. But, when Lady Lavinia turned to speak to one of the estate workers standing beside her, her husband's eyes were drawn to those of the woman sitting in the wheelchair opposite. And Olivia, sensitive to every nuance of the situation, glimpsed a raw emotion she had never before seen displayed.

It was over almost instantly. Her father came to his feet, to take charge of his wife's wheelchair, and Felicity looked up at him, her face alight with compassion. She knew how he was feeling, and she was showing she shared his grief; but the warmth between them was a passive thing, compared to the passion Olivia had intercepted.

And it shook her. As she followed her parents on to the stone path that led to the lych-gate, Olivia found she was trembling. And not just because she had caught Matthew's eyes upon her, with much the same kind of bitter anguish in their depths. Until that moment, she realised, she had always held out the hope that perhaps her grandmother had been mistaken, that maybe, somewhere, there was some other 'Matthew' whom her mother had known. Now, she no longer entertained such a belief. Whatever she might have thought of her grandmother for telling her, it was *true*. Her mother had had a relationship with Matthew's father, and she was the living proof.

Later that afternoon, Matthew cornered her in her father's study.

The funeral over, family and friends had returned to the farm, where a buffet lunch, prepared by Mrs Davis, was waiting. Not surprisingly, the house was soon filled to overflowing with the many mourners whom Harriet

Stoner had known through her work for church committees, but after three glasses of sherry Olivia had sought refuge away from the crowd, in the hope of avoiding the many expressions of sympathy she felt she didn't deserve.

Even so, she was restless, pacing about the stuffy room, regretting now her decision to stay on after the funeral. She had phoned Perry the night before, in the hope that he might reassure her, but he had been annoyed that she was staying in England. New York was her home now, he maintained, and her family hadn't cared about her all these years, so why should she care about them now?

Of course, she had tried to explain. She had told him about her mother's heart attack, and her subsequent disablement, but Perry had not been sympathetic. He was missing her, he said. She was neglecting the agency. That should be of more importance than something that had happened so long ago, and for which there was no solution now.

It wasn't what she had wanted to hear, she acknowledged. After talking to Matthew—after putting herself through the agony of remembering what had happened ten years ago—she had needed Perry's support, not his condemnation. She had been hoping to re-establish her links with the life she had now, but all Perry had done was leave her feeling even more confused.

Last night, she had been disturbed by the feelings Matthew still aroused inside her. She had wanted to prove to herself that she was exaggerating their importance, and that as soon as she heard Perry's voice she would come to her senses. But it hadn't happened that way. And today, after that incident at the funeral, she was very much afraid she was heading towards disaster.

Consequently, when the door opened and Matthew came into the room, she was in no mood to be conciliatory. 'What do you want?' she demanded irritably, as he closed the door behind him and leaned back against it. 'Just go away and leave me alone, Matt. I warn you, I'm not good company right now.'

Matthew took no notice. He just ran the palms of his hands down the panels of the door behind him, before pushing himself forward into the room. He had loosened the top two buttons of his shirt, and pulled his black tie away from his collar, but he still looked better than any man she had ever seen. And she still wanted him, she thought despairingly. The desire to slip her hands inside his collar and stroke the brown column of his throat was a burning temptation, and she turned her back on him to try and silence the forbidden clamouring of her senses.

'Are—are people leaving?' she asked offhandedly, picking up the glass she had carried into the study with her, and swallowing the remainder of its contents. That was four sherries she had had now, she warned herself, wondering if the wine was responsible for the appalling lack of control she seemed to have over her body. She had shed the jacket of her suit, but her arms inside the black chiffon blouse she was wearing were still too hot. And every time she looked at Matthew she could feel the beads of sweat trickling between her breasts.

'I don't know,' Matthew answered now, his hand taking the empty glass from hers, revealing that he had come to stand beside her. 'I don't particularly care, do you? I'm sorry the old lady's dead, but she was never any friend of mine.'

'No.' Olivia swallowed the urge to turn towards him, and looked away. Towards the window, this time, and the sun-bleached vegetation of the kitchen garden, where her mother grew the peas and carrots they had eaten at supper the previous evening.

'Nor yours either, if what you told me was true,' Matthew continued softly, lifting his hand to loop a tendril of hair behind her ear, and Olivia flinched away from him.

'What do you mean?' she exclaimed, incapable in that moment of remembering what she had said, and Matthew expelled his breath on a sigh.

'When she told me you'd been planning to leave all along,' he reminded her evenly. 'Correct me if I'm wrong, but I got the impression that wasn't the way it was.'

'Does it matter?' Olivia put a little more space between them, and leaned on the sill. The window was ajar, and the coolness that came through the gap was very welcome. 'It's so hot,' she added, half to herself, smoothing the moist skin in the hollow of her throat. 'There's no air.'

'It's the sherry,' remarked Matthew, coming to prop his hips on the sill beside her. 'You've been knocking it back pretty consistently since we got back from the service.'

'How do you know?' Olivia looked at him then, her eyes dark with indignation, and Matthew lifted his shoulders.

'I've been watching you.'

'You have no right to!'

'Don't I?' He arched a speculative brow, and Olivia could feel her heart pounding as she dragged her eyes away from his.

'No.'

'Liv.' His voice was persuasive now. 'Why did you really walk out on me? God—I've got to know!'

'You do know,' she retorted, in a constricted voice, concentrating on a bee, that was buzzing in and out of a head of cauliflower that had gone to seed. 'I—our relationship was getting too—heavy. You wanted to get married. I didn't.'

'I don't believe that.'

Matthew's response was driven from him, and Olivia had to hold on to the sill very tightly, in an effort to avoid the urge to console him. But when he gripped the edge of the sill and tipped his head back, to rest it against the window pane, the need to touch him became irresistible, and although she knew she would regret it later, she ran the palm of her hand across his taut knuckles.

His hand moved then, turning over to grasp hers, and
his fingers slid between her fingers in a totally sensuous
gesture. 'Liv,' he said hoarsely, and even though she
knew what she was doing was wrong she didn't pull away.
'I love you, Liv,' he muttered, lifting her hand to his
lips, and pressing his mouth against her palm. 'I always
have. I always will.'

'No——'

She tore her hand away from his then, pressing both
hands against her chest, as if he had done her some terrible injury. And that was how it felt, she thought, gazing
down at her balled fists. With that small action, he had
opened a wound that had never properly healed, and
now it was raw, and bleeding.

'For pity's sake, Liv,' he said now, getting up from
the window sill and coming towards her, and although
she backed away from him it was a futile gesture. He
caught her easily, and when he put out his hands and
gripped the curve of her neck she didn't resist him.

She thought he was going to kiss her, but he didn't.
Not then. He just pulled her into his arms and pressed
his face into the silky mass of her hair. And Olivia held
him, too, her arms around his waist, inside his jacket,
with only the fine silk of his shirt between her and his
warm flesh. Her cheek was against his chest, just beside
the loosened knot of his tie, and the musky smell of his
skin invaded her nostrils.

'God, do you know how good this feels?' he muttered, after a minute, and although Olivia was in total
agreement his words aroused her from the sensual stupor
of her senses.

'You're right,' she said, but when his hand moved to
her nape, to tip her face up to his, she pressed her hands
against his chest. 'I—have had too much to drink,' she
continued, knowing it was not what he had expected to
hear. 'I think you'd better let me go——'

Matthew's mouth contorted. 'You don't mean that.'

'I do mean it.' She succeeded in pushing him to arm's length. 'You forget—you're—married, and I—I am going to marry Perry——— '

'Like hell,' swore Matthew angrily, disposing of her resistance effortlessly, jerking her back against him so hard that she almost lost her breath. 'I won't let you marry that creep! I won't let you marry anyone! You're—*mine*.' And, forcing her to look at him, he covered her mouth with his.

Her eyes were open and so were his, so that she could see the raw passion in their depths. And then the hungry possession of his tongue in her mouth robbed her of all reason, and her lids wouldn't stay open any longer. Her world narrowed to encompass only the two of them; there was just Matthew's hands, and Matthew's lips, and the hard strength of Matthew's body straining against hers.

She sagged against him helplessly, clutching his shirt-front to prevent herself from falling as her knees gave way, and only realised she was hurting him when he took a sudden intake of breath.

Her eyes opened then, but her dilating pupils only solicited a muffled protest. 'It doesn't matter,' he said when she blinked her disbelief, and, releasing her mouth with reluctance, he shoved his hand between them, and dragged open the remaining buttons of his shirt. 'You grabbed a handful of hair, that's all,' he explained, his arm around her waist supporting her. 'And while you're welcome to strip me naked I'd rather you didn't skin me first.'

'Oh, *Matt*!'

His humour was so familiar to her, and although it was her chance to bring some sanity to the situation it had the opposite effect. Instead of drawing away from him, she cradled his face between her hands and studied him, as if she needed to commit his image to memory. But she knew every pore of his lean features, from the laughter-lines around his eyes to the muscle that pulsed below his jawline. She had once covered every inch of

face with kisses, and as she continued to look at him she
knew he was remembering that, too.

'Say it,' he said roughly, his hands sliding down her
back to the rounded swell of her buttocks. His hands
cupped their shapely curve, and as he brought her deliberately against him, she felt the hard ridge of his
arousal rising against her stomach. 'Say you love me,'
he added, taking hold of her skirt, and drawing it up,
so that he could touch her bare leg. 'You know you do.'
His hand moved higher, and she felt herself relaxing to
make it easier for him. 'Oh, God, Liv, I want you! Don't
pretend you're not ready for me, too——'

'Livvy! Livvy, where are you?'

Someone was calling her name, and although it seemed
to be coming from a great distance it was a persistent
aggravation. And, like a fly beating at the panes of her
consciousness, it eventually became too irritating to
ignore.

Which was just as well, thought Olivia later, realising
that both she and Matthew had been in danger of forgetting exactly where they were. Indeed, she fretted, if
her mother's voice hadn't interrupted them, there was
every possibility that she would have let him take her,
there, in her father's study, in full view of anyone who
might have ventured into the vegetable garden.

But being seen was not the worst of it, she knew. Her
own behaviour was what troubled her most. She had
allowed Matthew to touch her, knowing she had no right
to do so, neither legally nor morally.

In fact, it wasn't her mother who had found them
together. It was Mrs Davis, acting on her mother's
behalf, but evidently very interested in her own right.
Thank goodness her mother had called her name and
warned them, thought Olivia weakly, as Mrs Davis
opened the door. Although Matthew's shirt wasn't but-
toned beneath his hastily knotted tie, and Olivia was sure
her face was bare of all make-up, they were at opposite
sides of the room. Nevertheless, she wasn't at all con-

vinced that the housekeeper was deceived. The way she
looked at them gave Olivia an anxious feeling in the pit
of her stomach, and she was relieved when Matthew took
the initiative.

'Yes?' he said coolly, and watching him Olivia would
never have believed that moments before he had been at
the mercy of his senses. 'Did you want something?'

In spite of her avid curiosity, Mrs Davis was not indifferent to Matthew's position, and her thin lips curled
back over her teeth in an ingratiating smile. 'Er—Mrs
Stoner was looking for her daughter, Mr Matthew,' she
explained, but, unable to withstand his narrow-eyed
stare, she looked at Olivia again. 'People are leaving,
Miss Stoner. I think your mother would like you to join
the rest of the family to say goodbye.'

'Would she?' Olivia licked her lips, and cast a nervous
look in Matthew's direction. 'Oh—very well.'

'You can tell Mrs Stoner that Olivia will be with her
shortly,' Matthew retorted, getting up from the desk. He
had propped his hips against the worn mahogany rim
as Mrs Davis opened the door, but now he went towards
her with every indication of seeing her outside.

But Olivia knew she couldn't let him. They *mustn't*
be alone again, and, abandoning her stance by the
window, she hurried across the floor. 'I'll come now,
Mrs Davis,' she said, and before Matthew could prevent
her she brushed past them both.

Her mother was in her wheelchair, at the end of the
passage, and Olivia went towards her eagerly, desperate
to avoid Matthew's censure. She was afraid he might
come after her, and she didn't think she could handle
him right now. She needed time to gather her scattered
senses before she saw him again; time to assimilate her
position, and find some convincing reason why they
mustn't see one another again.

'Are you all right, Livvy?'

Mrs Stoner looked up at her elder daughter with some
concern, and Olivia took a deep breath before saying
tautly, 'As I'll ever be, I suppose.'

Felicity Stoner frowned. 'Why? What's wrong? Have you and Matthew had a row?'

'Have we had a row?' Olivia caught her breath. That her mother, of all people, should ask that! But, 'No,' she answered, wondering why she didn't feel more animosity towards her mother. After all, she was to blame, wasn't she? 'No, we haven't been—rowing.'

'Oh, good.'

Mrs Stoner half turned her chair, but before she could move away Olivia said unsteadily, 'Tell me—tell me, why didn't—Matthew's wife come to the funeral? I thought she would.'

'Helen?' Her mother's mouth tightened. 'Hasn't Matthew told you about Helen yet?'

'Told me? Told me what?' Olivia moved round the chair to gaze down at her. 'What about her?'

'Oh, not now, darling.' Mrs Stoner shook her head. 'And if Matt hasn't told you himself, I don't think it's my place——'

'What about her?' repeated Olivia grimly, and her mother gave an exaggerated sigh.

'We can't talk about it now,' she said. 'We simply don't have the time. Ask me later, after everyone has gone.'

Olivia caught her lower lip between her teeth. 'They—they are still married, aren't they?'

But, even as she asked the question she realised that both Matthew and Mrs Davis were coming along the passage towards them. And, clearly, her mother had realised it, too.

'Later, Livvy,' she said, squeezing her daughter's hand, and, tapping the arm of her chair, she added, 'Take me into the drawing-room, dear. Your father's waiting for us.'

CHAPTER TEN

OLIVIA sat back on her heels, and surveyed the patch of garden she had just weeded. It definitely looked a lot better but, short of rain, the soil still looked dry and flaky. It was a wonder anything at all grew in such conditions, she thought. But, however hot it was, weeds always seemed to flourish, taking what little moisture there was for themselves, and leaving the plants to perish.

She looked down at her hands. A week ago, when she left New York, her nails had been neatly filed, and painted with a pearl lustre. Now, they were bare of any polish, and caked with earth into the bargain.

Still, she had gained a certain amount of satisfaction from working in the garden. It made her feel useful— something she had not felt since she landed in England. And it also served to expunge her frustration, and ease the aching need inside her that she knew could never be assuaged.

It was three days now since the funeral; three days since Matthew had walked out of the house, without even telling her goodbye. Not that she regretted his abstinence, she told herself. The less she and Matthew said to one another, the better. But she couldn't deny that not seeing him had caused something to shrivel up inside her. And, despite her best efforts, whenever a car did come to the door and it wasn't Matthew she suffered a small defeat.

Of course, she could hardly blame him for keeping away. She had done nothing to endear herself in his eyes. That encounter in the study on the day of the funeral had achieved nothing. It had only proved to him, once and for all, that she was just as selfish as he had thought.

Oh, she could argue that he had no room to talk; that he was still married, and therefore in no real position to criticise her morals. But the fact remained, she had let him think she cared about him. *Think?* She pulled a wry face. There was no *think* about it. She did still care about him. But that was no excuse for what she had done. No excuse at all.

Yet why should she take all the blame, when every time he came near her she seemed incapable of rational thought? She was the one who deserved to be pitied. It was her soul she was damning to perdition.

And, so far as Matthew's relationship with Helen was concerned, she had only her mother's word that everything was not as it should be. The point was only academic, after all, but Mrs Stoner had explained that Helen didn't just work at the Berrenger Stables these days, she *lived* there. Had lived there for some time, in fact.

Which meant that their marriage wasn't working, but didn't alter her position at all, Olivia reflected bitterly. Oh, she couldn't deny that the knowledge that Matthew was not living in a state of married bliss appealed to the baser side of her nature. But, in all honesty, she didn't wish that for him. She loved him, for God's sake! She wanted him to be happy. The trouble was, she had the instinctive feeling that neither of them could be happy apart.

Life was a bitch! she thought painfully, getting to her feet now, and brushing the soil from her fingers. What she should do—what she ought to have done ten years ago—was have it out with her mother; ask her how she could have allowed their relationship to continue, knowing what she did. Only Felicity Stoner could explain how she had appeased her conscience all these years, and then, maybe, she would find a way to appease her own.

But Olivia knew she couldn't do that. What good would it do, after all? It couldn't help her. And it might do irreparable harm to the family. Not to mention her mother's health. All she should do was go back to New

York, and Perry. Accept, once and for all, that she and Matthew didn't have a future together, and stop playing with fire.

Footsteps sounded on the path behind her, and she turned round in surprise. Her mother was resting, her father and Andrew were down in the fields somewhere, and even Mrs Davis had gone into the village. She had thought she was alone in the house, and her eyes widened in dismay when she recognised her visitor.

It was ten years since she had seen Helen Berrenger— no, *Ryan*, she corrected herself tautly, but she hadn't changed. Helen had always been tall, and thin, and slightly masculine in appearance, preferring riding breeches to jeans or trousers, and linen shirts to cotton. Her hair was her only concession to her femininity, and now, as then, she wore it long and straight, and tied back with a leather cord. Olivia had always thought she was quite attractive, in an angular sort of way, but her opinion had always been coloured by Matthew's, and in those days he had had no time for her.

But now she was walking along the path towards her, and Olivia thought how ironic it was that Helen should see her at her worst. She couldn't imagine why she should have come to see her, but she wished she had been more prepared. Ten years in one of the most sophisticated cities in the world should have given her the advantage. But in a dust-smeared T-shirt and an old pair of Andrew's jeans she had the uneasy feeling that the reverse was true.

Smoothing her hands over the seat of the jeans, she prepared herself to meet the challenge. Whatever reason Helen had for coming here, she couldn't believe it was a charitable one. As girls, they had only known one another distantly. It was inconceivable, now that Helen was married to Matthew, that they could have anything in common.

Except Matthew, a small voice jeered inside her, and Olivia's stomach tightened unpleasantly. It wasn't sensible, she knew, but the image of Matthew making love to Helen made her skin creep. How would Helen look, with her hair spread out all over the pillow? she wondered. Had Matthew buried his face in its softness, as he had done with hers, and caressed it with his lips...

'Hello.' Helen had halted a few feet away, a constrained smile splitting her thin features. 'I hope I'm not disturbing you.'

'Oh—no.' Olivia found it difficult to hide her surprise at the other woman's cordiality. Somehow, she had got it into her head that Helen had heard she was back, and had come to warn her off Matthew. But Helen's attitude didn't seem to be aggressive, which seemed to confound that theory.

Even so, it was possible she was hiding her true feelings. People like the Berrengers did that, she remembered. And the Ryans, too, she appended, recalling Matthew's father's behaviour at her grandmother's funeral. Not to forget her own mother, she thought wryly. Felicity Stoner was a past mistress at the art.

'Um—can I help you?' Olivia ventured now, incapable of thinking of any reason, other than Matthew, that might have brought Helen here. She had to know they had been seeing one another. Even though the Berrenger Stables were some miles from Lower Mychett, news of that sort travelled fast.

'I hope so,' Helen responded now. And then, as if as uncomfortable with the situation, as Olivia was herself, she directed her attention towards the garden. 'You look as if you've been busy.'

'Yes. Yes, I have.' Olivia looked down at the patch where she had been working, too, and noticed a stem of milkweed she had overlooked. But her mind wasn't really on the results of her labours. She just wished Helen would get to the point.

'I don't suppose you've had much time for gardening, while you've been living in America,' Helen continued, evidently in no hurry to do so. 'New York, wasn't it? Quite a change from Lower Mychett, I should think.'

'Quite a change,' agreed Olivia, gesturing for Helen to walk back along the path. 'Um—shall we go into the house? I'd like to wash my hands.'

'Oh! Oh, yes, of course.'

Helen turned obediently away, and Olivia followed her tall, athletic figure round to the back door of the farmhouse. But, once there, Helen hung back to allow the other girl to precede her inside, and Olivia hesitated only a moment before doing so.

'So,' she said at last, after washing her hands at the sink, while Helen hovered in the doorway. 'What can I do for you?'

Helen licked her lips, and watching her, Olivia's nerves jangled. For goodness' sake, get on with it, she thought, thrusting the towel on which she had dried her hands aside. It was obviously because of Matthew that she was here, and the only question remaining was from whom Helen had gleaned her information. Perhaps someone had seen them, that day after the funeral. Goodness knew, neither of them had been in any state to notice!

'It's—it's not easy for me to talk about this,' Helen said at last, and Olivia could only feel a sense of relief that apparently she was going to try. 'I—I suppose you know my father—died—just after you went away.'

Olivia blinked. It was not what she had been expecting to hear, and for a moment she just stared at her. But then, gathering her wits, she nodded. 'I—did hear something, yes.'

'Something? Or everything?' enquired Helen drily. 'From your expression, I'd say the latter was true.'

'Well——' Now it was Olivia's turn to prevaricate. 'I heard he died in tragic circumstances——'

'Yes.' Helen bent her head. 'Tragic circumstances. That about covers it.'

'I was—very sorry,' murmured Olivia awkwardly, wondering what any of this had to do with her, and then biting her lip when Helen gave her a disbelieving look.

'Why should you be sorry?' Revealing the first trace of animosity she had shown since she came here, Helen regarded her coldly now, and Olivia made a helpless gesture.

'No—no reason,' she murmured placatingly. 'Um——' She glanced behind her. 'Would you like some coffee? Or a cold drink——?'

'Nothing.' Helen shook her head, and Olivia wondered why offering her sympathy should have elicited quite such a response. 'But—I'd like to sit down, if I may? Would you mind?'

'Of course not.' Olivia felt guilty for not having invited her to do so. But she remained standing, preferring the freedom to move at will.

'Thank you.' Helen subsided into a chair at the table, and then looked up at the other girl. 'Won't you join me?'

In spite of her reticence Olivia could think of no reason why not, and, shaking her head a little bewilderedly, she pulled out a chair from the table, and did so. But her knees were shaking, and she crossed her legs so that Helen shouldn't notice.

'All right.' With the conditions to her apparent liking, Helen rested her arms on the table and looked at her unwilling confidante. 'I'll accept that your sympathies were well meant. But you'll have to forgive me. I'm a little touchy where my father's death is concerned.'

Olivia gave a small smile, but she was rapidly coming to the conclusion that Helen was, if not unbalanced, then at least a little irrational. She could see no earthly reason why she should have come here, if not to approach her about Matthew, but so far Helen hadn't even mentioned him.

'Anyway,' Helen was continuing, and Olivia endeavoured to concentrate on what she was saying, 'it is true to say that—the rumours that were spread about him after his death were not entirely without foundation.'

'No?' Olivia ran her hand into the damp hair at her nape, wondering what was coming now.

'No.' Helen squared her shoulders. 'He was having—financial difficulties. That much is true. Indeed, I'm sure they contributed to his—accident.'

'You are?'

'Yes.' Helen nodded. 'He wasn't paying proper attention to what he was doing. Daddy would never have clipped that fence if he hadn't been distracted.'

'I see.'

Olivia's response was polite, but as if realising she was losing the other girl's attention Helen hurried on, 'It *was* an accident, you see. Oh, people said it wasn't. They said Daddy had taken his own life, because he was in debt, and by doing so he was enabling me to collect the insurance money, but that wasn't true!'

'No.'

'You do believe me, don't you?'

Helen was gazing at her anxiously now, and Olivia could only nod her head, and assure her that she did. 'Anyway,' she added, in an effort to divert her, 'that was all over a long time ago. It doesn't really matter now, does it——?'

'Yes, it does.' Helen leaned across the table. 'It matters a lot. It was why Matthew married me, you see. He didn't love me. Not really. He was just reacting to the fact that you had gone away, and he felt sorry for me.'

Olivia's mouth felt parched. 'Oh—I'm sure——' she began, but once again Helen interrupted her.

'It's true.' Helen took a deep breath. 'You have to believe me. There were—complications, you see. With the insurance money. As I said before, there were rumours, and insurance companies don't like paying out huge sums of money if there are any doubts.'

Olivia managed to nod. 'I can believe that.'

'So you see, they were far more prepared to take a lenient view of the situation with the Ryans behind me, and Matthew and I—well, we had always been friends, as you know.'

Olivia became aware that her fingers were twisting together, and to prevent this from continuing she sat on her hands. But she didn't know how much more of this she could take, and adopting what she hoped was an unrevealing expression she said tightly, 'I'm sure this is all very interesting. But—I don't understand why you're telling me.'

'Because I want you to ask Matthew to get a divorce,' declared Helen coolly, and Olivia slumped back in her chair, feeling utterly dumbfounded.

'I can see you're surprised,' Helen went on, after a minute, and Olivia thought how inadequate that expression was to describe how she was feeling. 'But— you have to believe me when I say it's what we both want really.'

'What you both want?' Olivia swallowed, barely capable of coherent thought, and Helen gave a nervous laugh.

'Yes.' She hesitated for a moment, and then went on, 'It's difficult for me to say this, but I don't love Matthew either. Oh, I'm grateful to him. I'll always be grateful to him. But I think the time has come for me to take my life into my own hands. Matthew still thinks I can't manage on my own, but I can. And I'm hoping you'll be able to persuade him, for all our sakes.'

Olivia stared at her aghast. 'You expect me to——'

'Well, you can't deny you're still attracted to one another,' put in Helen quickly. 'As soon as I heard you were coming back for your grandmother's funeral, I knew that you and Matthew——'

'Don't—don't say any more!'

Olivia was hardly aware she had spoken aloud until Helen faltered, her thin, aristocratic features mirroring the indignation she was feeling. Until then, the disbelief Olivia was feeling that they should be having this conversation had kept her mute, but now a feeling of raw betrayal was sweeping over her. How could Helen come here and say these things to her? It was unbelievable!

'I don't know why you're looking at me like that,' Helen declared huffily, recovering her equilibrium. 'You can't pretend that you and Matthew haven't—been alone

together. Why, Enid said she thought you both looked
as guilty as Judas when she found you——'

'*Enid!*' Olivia's face showed her distaste. 'Do you
mean Enid Davis?'

Helen hesitated, as if regretting mentioning the other
woman's name, but then she evidently decided it wasn't
worth worrying over. 'I suppose so,' she replied,
shrugging her shoulders. 'She's your mother's housekeeper, isn't she?'

Olivia got up from her chair and walked across to the
window above the sink. Her mind was in a turmoil, and
it was incredibly difficult not to demand that Helen get
out of the house, immediately. How could she discuss
her marriage to Matthew so dispassionately? It was as
if it was a temporary inconvenience that she wished to
be free of.

And yet, although that was true, Olivia couldn't help
thinking what this could have meant to her and Matthew.
If they had had the right to a future together, she might
well have jumped at Helen's offer. She had guessed he
had married Helen on the rebound, but until now she
had had no idea of the other factors involved. But the
other woman's explanation had done much to define his
motives ten years ago, and in normal circumstances she
would have forgiven him willingly.

It occurred to her then that, in effect—if not in the
eyes of God—she could pretend that these were normal
circumstances. Her grandmother's death had destroyed
the only obstacle that had stood in their path. If her
mother hadn't objected to her relationship with Matthew
ten years ago, why would she object now? And
Matthew's father—*her father*—didn't even know he had
a daughter...

She caught her breath. Dear God, she thought sickly,
what was she thinking? Helen had come to her with her
preposterous suggestion, and in so doing, she had opened
Olivia's mind to—*corruption*. There was no other word
for it. She had actually been considering breaking every
law known to God and man. And why? Because no one

knew—or cared—that she was old Matthew Ryan's daughter.

But she knew, she reminded herself bitterly. And even if she wasn't flesh of Harriet Stoner's flesh, she had absorbed enough of her teachings throughout her life to know she couldn't go through with it.

Still, the idea that Helen should have come here to ask her to intercede on her behalf was incredible. And yet, if what Helen said was true, it did have a twisted kind of logic. And she was beginning to realise that Helen was anything but illogical.

Licking her lips, she turned, gripping the drainer behind her for support. 'W-why don't *you* ask Matt—Matthew for a divorce?' she asked.

'Do you think I haven't?' Helen got up from the table, then, and although Olivia was half afraid she was going to come across the room towards her, the other woman merely rested her hands on the back of her chair. 'Of course I've asked him,' she added. 'But as I said earlier, Matthew is an—honourable man. He still thinks I couldn't manage without him!'

Olivia frowned. 'But—you do—live apart, don't you?'

'Well—yes.' Helen shrugged. 'But that means nothing in a court of law.'

'A court of law!' Olivia was confused. 'I'm afraid I——'

'Oh, forget it,' said Helen swiftly, and once again Olivia had the distinct impression her visitor felt she had said too much. 'I—I just thought you might feel as I do. That—Matthew had sacrificed his own happiness long enough.'

Put like that, Olivia couldn't argue with it, and as if seeing the acknowledgement in her eyes Helen made her final appeal. 'Matthew doesn't know I'm here, of course,' she said. 'And he mustn't. If he thought I had approached you, he'd feel utterly humiliated. But I wanted you to know that I'd do nothing to prevent you two from getting back together, and I also know that if

Matthew thought it was what you wanted he'd ask me
for a divorce tomorrow!'

Helen left, as she had come, on the rather temperamental stallion that had apparently brought her, which
explained why Olivia hadn't heard her arrival. Not that
the other woman's means of getting there was of any
importance. Compared to the upheaval she had caused
Olivia, how Helen had actually got here didn't warrant
consideration.

The idea of going on with her gardening was no longer
appealing either, and Olivia poured herself a glass of
orange juice and tried to relax. But even half an hour
later she was still in a state of some distraction, and her
mother's appearance from the bedroom didn't make
things any easier.

'Did I hear voices earlier?' Mrs Stoner enquired,
wheeling herself across the floor, and switching on the
kettle. 'I thought I did. Was it Enid?'

'No.' Olivia's response was scarcely audible, and at
her mother's raised brows she added, 'It was Helen.'

'Helen?' Her mother looked as surprised as Olivia had
done, when she first recognised her visitor. 'Helen was
here!'

'Mmm.' Olivia couldn't quite meet her mother's gaze,
and Felicity Stoner frowned.

'So?' She arched brows very like her daughter's. 'What
did she want?'

'To see me,' said Olivia offhandedly. 'Um—did you
have a good rest?'

'Olivia!'

Her mother's use of her name was impatient, and
Olivia sighed.

'All right. If you must know, she came to tell me that
Mrs Davis has been gossiping about—about Matthew
and me.'

'Enid!' Mrs Stoner was evidently shocked. 'What has
she been saying?'

'Oh——' Inwardly Olivia groaned. 'Just that she found us together. You remember. The day of the funeral.'

'And what did Helen say about that?'

That she wants me to ask Matthew to get a divorce! Olivia answered silently, but then, realising she couldn't confide in her mother, she shrugged. 'Not a lot.' She paused, and then added, rather unevenly, 'Do you know why she and Matt got married?'

'Well, I know why she married Matthew,' responded Mrs Stoner quietly. 'I'm not quite so clear as to why he married her.' She looked at her daughter, and Olivia wished she found it easier to dissemble. 'He was on the rebound from you, of course. That could have tipped the balance.'

'From me!'

Olivia felt her nails digging into her palms, and she longed to ask her mother how she could sit there and say such a thing, without any apparent trace of conscience. Didn't she have any idea what she was condoning? Didn't she care? How could anyone live with Harriet Stoner all those years and not feel the warning hand of fate?

'Yes, from you,' Felicity said now, allowing the kettle to turn itself off again, without making any attempt to make some tea. 'You knew how Matt felt about you. Oh, I realise you were young, and perhaps you weren't ready to settle down, but you can have been in no doubt that that was what Matt expected.'

Olivia stared at her. 'But,' she said, choosing her words with care, 'don't you think our—relationship—was a little—unwise——'

'Because of the differences between you?' broke in her mother quickly. 'Oh, no. I don't think so. You may not have been Lady Lavinia's first choice as a wife for her son, but Matt's father was always very fond of you, you know that.'

Olivia's throat constricted. 'Well, he would be, wouldn't he?' she said, in a strangled voice, but instead of the reaction she had half expected her mother laughed.

'You mean because he always had a weakness for a pretty face?' she exclaimed lightly. 'Well, yes, I suppose——'

'No. I meant because—because I was *your* daughter,' said Olivia, feeling like the worst kind of traitor, but instead of looking anxious her mother only sighed.

'I wondered if you'd ever heard that old story,' she said, her expression turning wistful. 'Yes. Matthew's father and I were—friends, years ago. I dare say he does see a likeness between us.'

And not just between us, thought Olivia wretchedly, only she didn't have the nerve to say it. Her mother had said enough, after all. She had admitted that she and Matthew's father had known one another. She didn't know her daughter had seen the letters, but she didn't need to. Taken together, the two things were irrefutable.

'Anyway, I shall speak to Enid Davis, when I get the chance,' Felicity continued now, and Olivia was half relieved to have the initiative taken from her. 'But Helen must know that you shouldn't rely on gossip. I hope she didn't upset you, my dear. I fear Helen knows her days as Matthew's wife are numbered.'

CHAPTER ELEVEN

OLIVIA rang Agnes Reina that evening, and confirmed that the other woman was coping very well without her. 'But I have to tell you that Perry's been in and out of the office during the last couple of days, asking me if I've heard from you, and if I know when you're coming back,' Agnes added ruefully. 'For goodness' sake, put the poor man out of his misery. Tell him how long you're planning to stay.'

'Not—not much longer,' said Olivia cautiously, re-alising she was only putting off booking her return flight because of Matthew. It was crazy, she knew, particularly after what she had learned that afternoon, but the idea of putting several thousand miles between them again was tearing her to pieces.

'Well, hurray,' said Agnes, laughing. 'I'll tell him, shall I? Or would you rather do it yourself?'

'No. No, you tell him, Agnes,' replied Olivia weakly. 'Um—just say I expect to be back within the week. I'll let you know the exact day later.'

'OK.'

Agnes rang off, but Olivia sat for some time staring at the phone after she had done so. Somehow the agency, and the life she had led in New York, seemed so remote— unreal, almost—and she knew she had no real desire to go back there. She was even playing with the idea of starting an agency here in England, so that she could divide her time between the two, but the dangers in-herent in that were colossal. She should never have come back, she thought, for the umpteenth time. She had thought the fire was dead, but it had only been smouldering. Now she had blown life into it again, and like a forest blaze it was rapidly getting out of control.

The next morning Olivia got a call from Lady Lavinia Ryan. It came while her father was at home, having his morning break, and he answered the phone. 'It's Lady Lavinia,' he said, coming out of his study, looking a little red-faced. 'She wants to speak to you, Livvy. You'd better take it in here.'

'For me?'

Olivia's stomach plunged, and a little of what she was feeling must have shown in her face, because her father said, a little harshly, 'Just watch what you say, girl. I don't want you upsetting the Ryans again.'

Olivia's eyes widened, and she exchanged an indignant look with her mother, but she had no choice about taking the call. So far as Robert Stoner was concerned, it was a royal summons.

All the same, she was surprised when Matthew's mother quickly dispensed with the preliminaries, and invited her to Rycroft for supper that evening. 'I hope you'll come, Olivia,' she said, and Olivia knew it was in the nature of a command. People didn't refuse invitations to Rycroft. And if her father thought she had, she would never hear the end of it.

'Well——' she began, trying desperately to think of some legitimate reason why she should refuse, but Lady Lavinia was not prepared to listen to her excuses.

'I think you owe it to us to come, Olivia,' she said, making a refusal that much more difficult. 'We don't want anyone to think that we bear any grudges, do we?'

Olivia's lips parted. 'No.'

'Good. I'm glad you see it that way. We'll expect you at seven-thirty. Informal dress, of course.'

Olivia spent the remainder of the day, until it was time to get ready to go to Rycroft, trying to anticipate why Lady Lavinia should have issued her invitation. As far as she could see, there was no earthly reason why the Ryans should want to entertain her, and the prospect of meeting Matthew's father again, knowing what she did, was not appealing. What if her grandmother had been wrong? What if Matthew's father did know she was his

daughter? Oh, God! What would she do if he brought
the subject up?

But, as she dressed to go out that evening, she refused
to consider that eventuality. She couldn't believe that if
Mr Ryan did know he wouldn't have done something
about it. A person like that wouldn't just ignore his responsibilities—*would he*?

Deciding what to wear was the least of her problems.
Because she had never intended to stay on after the funeral, the few clothes she had brought with her provided
little choice. It was either the silk suit she had worn on
the day of the funeral, or trousers and a casual top; and
while Lady Lavinia had said informal dress, Olivia
couldn't see her sitting down to supper in trousers. Consequently, she chose the suit, teaming it with a cream
vest, instead of the black one she had worn to church.

A shower had left her hair soft and silky, the perm
she had had some weeks before gentling into waves about
her unnaturally pale face. And, noticing how pale she
was, she added a trace of blusher to her cheekbones to
lessen the impact. The last thing she wanted was for the
Ryans to think she was afraid to meet them—even if she
was!

It had been arranged that her father should run her
to Rycroft, but when she came downstairs at a quarter
past seven she found Matthew lounging in the drawing-
room, talking to her parents. He was the last person she
had expected to see, and, far from appearing pale, a
wave of hot colour swept into her cheeks when she saw
him. Somehow she had got it into her head that he had
had no part in his mother's invitation, and although she
knew he still lived at Rycroft she had half imagined he
wouldn't be there tonight.

'Matt's come to take you to Rycroft,' her father remarked, as if an explanation was necessary. He gave his
daughter a speaking look. 'Isn't that kind of him?'

Olivia moistened her lips. 'Very kind,' she said, responding to the warning in her father's expression. 'But
I hope you told him it wasn't necessary.'

'I thought I'd save you having to drive home alone,' averred Matthew evenly. 'I didn't realise your father was going to bring you.'

'Really?'

Olivia knew there was an edge to her voice, but she couldn't help it, and Robert Stoner elaborated. 'Matt thought you'd be driving yourself,' he declared. 'But I explained you got your licence in the States.'

'I see.'

Olivia's colour was subsiding, but her heart was still sending the blood pounding through her veins, and she was amazed that no one else could hear it. It seemed deafening to her.

'OK.' Matthew put the empty glass he had been holding aside, and came lithely to his feet. He was wearing dark colours tonight—black trousers, and a dark grey shirt, open at the neck to reveal the brown column of his throat. Ten years ago his mother would have insisted he wore a tie, even for an informal dinner at home, Olivia reflected irrelevantly, but evidently times had changed. 'Shall we go?'

Do I have a choice? Olivia countered, but only to herself. With her father watching her like a hawk, and her mother displaying a genuine pleasure that she was going out for the evening, she couldn't spoil their enjoyment with her grudging comments. Besides, Lady Lavinia had probably asked Matthew to come and fetch her. She couldn't believe he had come here of his own volition. Not after the way she had behaved on the day of the funeral.

Outside, the Mercedes in which he had picked her up from the airport was waiting, and Matthew swung open the passenger door with cool civility before walking round to get in beside her. Then, with a friendly wave for her father, who had accompanied them to the door, he set the powerful estate car in motion.

Beyond the courtyard in front of the house, a short drive gave on to the lane that led to the village. It was an uneven track at the best of times, and the dry spell, following on a period of rain, had left corrugated grooves in its surface. But the Mercedes handled them magnificently, its suspension ironing out all but the most rugged furrows. And Olivia, compelled to make some effort to break the uneasy silence that seemed in danger of continuing, murmured ruefully, 'This can't be doing your car any good, coming down here twice or three times in as many days.'

'It's four days since I was here last,' replied Matthew, without expression, and Olivia realised his cordiality towards her didn't extend outside her parents' presence.

'Nevertheless——' she persisted, prepared to pursue it, but the look he gave her made her change her mind, and she looked out of the window instead. It was obvious he had no desire to debate anything with her, and she told herself she was glad. This way, she was not going to have to contend with him as well as his parents.

The journey to Rycroft took a little less than fifteen minutes, but by the time Matthew brought the car to a halt before the rambling old manor house Olivia was wishing she had persevered in her efforts to talk to him. She badly needed an ally, and no amount of self-justification could wholly assuage the way she had treated him.

The engine died as he turned off the ignition, but before he could get out of the car, Olivia touched his arm. 'Matt——'

'Well?'

His response was barely encouraging, and she had the feeling he wouldn't have answered at all if he hadn't been aware, as she was, that other eyes could be on them.

'Do——' She choked, and started again. 'D-do you know why your mother's invited me here?' she ventured, and Matthew paused to regard her with cool-eyed indifference.

'What's the matter?' he enquired. 'Got cold feet?'

Olivia pressed her lips together. 'Yes,' she said at last, deciding not to prevaricate. 'Yes. As a matter of fact, I have. Are you surprised?'

'Nothing about you ever surprises me,' retorted Matthew coldly, thrusting open his door. 'Come on. As far as I know, you're not about to face a firing squad.'

'And that's supposed to reassure me?' exclaimed Olivia, somewhat bitterly, and in spite of himself Matthew stayed in this seat.

'No one's going to embarrass you,' he replied wearily. 'Least of all me.' And Olivia's heart twisted at the dead expression in his eyes.

'Matt,' she began unwisely, 'about—about the other day——'

But evidently there were limits to how far he was prepared to go, and Matthew's mouth was grim when he came round the car to yank open her door. 'Forget it,' he said, and those few moments of tolerance might never have been. 'I have,' he added bleakly. 'Shall we go in?'

Olivia got out of the car with obvious reluctance. If it hadn't been for her father, she was sure she would have asked Matthew to take her home again. She didn't feel at all well, and the idea of sitting down to supper, *of actually swallowing food*, was nauseating. If nothing else, her grandmother had appreciated the position she was in. No one else seemed to.

But she was here now, and she had to go through with it, and, looking up at the wistaria-clad walls of the house, she thought how unchanging some things were. There had been a house on this land for hundreds of years, and although the present incumbent only owed its origins to the turn of the eighteenth century, it had a timeless quality. Of course, it had been added to over the years by its subsequent owners, and although it was substantially Georgian in design its raffish appearance possessed more charm than elegance. Nevertheless, it had beauty, and character, and Olivia had always liked coming here.

Maybe because this was her real heritage, she reflected bitterly, but somehow the thought lacked conviction. She was the product of her environment, not her heritage. A test case, if there ever was one.

Mrs Platt, the Ryans' housekeeper, was waiting in the open doorway, and her plump cheeks flushed with becoming colour when Olivia revealed she remembered her name. 'It's good to see you again, Miss Stoner,' she responded, closing the heavy door behind them, and Olivia wondered when she had graduated from being called by her Christian name to the more formal salutation.

'Are my mother and father in the library?'

Matthew was behind her, and Olivia moved aside to let him lead the way. Not that she didn't remember where the library was, of course, she thought unwillingly. Matthew had once made love to her there, while his parents were holidaying in the South of France——

'Yes. They're waiting for you, Mr Matt,' Mrs Platt answered, fortunately interrupting Olivia's train of thought. But it was difficult to dispel the memories here, when there were so many to haunt her.

'Thanks.'

Matthew's smile was free of artifice and, watching him with the housekeeper, Olivia thought how carelessly she had once accepted his affection. He had used to smile at her like that, she remembered, his love enveloping her in a protecting cloak. She had taken so much for granted, in those halcyon days. Was it just because she was young, or had they really cared that much for one another?

As Matthew led the way along the hall to the library she tried to concentrate her attention on the house. This corridor, with its long windows overlooking the lawns and shrubbery at the front of the house, was usually called the gallery. Because of the many paintings hung between the windows, Matthew had explained. Paintings of long dead inhabitants of Rycroft; though not all of them were his father's ancestors, he had assured her. Everyone knew the Ryans had only owned the estate since the middle of the last century. All the same, Olivia used to fancy she could see Matthew's likeness in a handsome young courtier, dressed in Tudor garb.

Tonight, however, she had no time to study the paintings, even if she would have liked to. Matthew's parents were waiting, and he paused at the heavy door to the library, allowing her to catch up with him.

'Don't look so scared,' he said roughly, as if compelled to offer a support he had no real wish to give, and Olivia closed her eyes. Damn them, she thought bitterly: her mother and Matthew's father. They had really screwed up their children's lives.

'Olivia.'

The door was open now, and Matthew's father was coming forward to take her limp hand in a welcoming grip. He smiled, and she made an effort to respond, but her enthusiasm was lacking, and he must have sensed it.

'Hello, Olivia.'

Lady Lavinia was behind her husband, and Olivia managed to put a little more feeling into her expression. After all, it wasn't Lady Lavinia's fault. She was just another innocent victim.

'Hello,' she answered, managing to include them both in her greeting. 'I hope we haven't kept you waiting.'

'Would you like a drink?'

Matthew's voice was achingly familiar, extracting her from prolonged politenesses, and giving her a reason to cross the room to his side.

'Um—a dry sherry, if you have it,' she said, her eyes meeting his without volition. She couldn't help wondering what she would have done if he hadn't been here. Where the Ryans were concerned, she still felt like a schoolgirl.

'Matthew's been telling us you're a successful businesswoman these days,' his father declared approvingly, and, taking a reassuring sip of her sherry, Olivia turned to face him.

'I run a small agency,' she admitted deprecatingly, suddenly noticing how much older Matthew's father looked. On the day of the funeral she had been more concerned with his behaviour than his appearance, but now she could see the changes his circumstances had wrought.

And yet he was still amazingly cheerful, she acknowledged, remembering the way he had always treated her with kindness and respect. Of course, with hindsight, it was possible to regard his friendliness towards her as a belated sense of guilt towards her mother, but Olivia preferred not to think of it that way. Biased she might be, but in her opinion Matthew's father was one of nature's gentlemen. Which was ironic really, considering he had behaved in a most ungentlemanly fashion towards her mother.

She wondered if there was any resemblance between them. She could see none, but perhaps she was just being optimistic. Still, if anyone might have been expected to notice, surely it would have been him. Yet his attitude towards her seemed just as impartial as ever.

'An agency for child-minders, I understand,' Lady Lavinia remarked now, and Olivia thought how typical it was of Matthew's mother to make it sound so trivial. She and her grandmother were two of a kind, she reflected drily.

'For nannies,' she amended, mildly, and Lady Lavinia arched an enquiring brow.

'But you were not trained as a nanny,' she pointed out smoothly, and Olivia lost a little of her nervousness as she went on to explain that, whatever her own lack of qualifications, the agency dealt only with fully qualified nurses.

'Well, anyway, I think Olivia's done very well,' said Matthew's father, inviting her to take a seat. 'I'm a great admirer of entrepreneurs, in any field. I wish I had had ideas like that.'

'I can't see you running an agency for nursemaids,' put in Matthew mildly, lightening the situation, and everyone laughed at the incongruity.

'Even so...'

Mr Ryan grimaced, and went off to get himself another Scotch and soda, and Lady Lavinia took the opportunity to ask Olivia if her parents were well, and bearing up in the present unhappy circumstances.

It was comparatively easy to talk about her parents, Olivia found. In spite of Matthew's father's past relationship with her mother, telling them what she knew about her grandmother's death was not controversial. It nicely filled the time between her arrival and Mrs Platt's announcement that the meal was ready, and when she sat down at the table she was almost ready to believe she had been worrying unnecessarily.

The food was impeccably served, as always. Olivia didn't know who had prepared the meal, but she actually enjoyed it, chatting with Matthew's father as if their relationship was no different from what it had ever been. It was the only way to cope with it, she realised. If she could pretend it had never happened, perhaps she could eventually find some peace of mind. But not with Matthew, she reminded herself tautly. Never with Matthew.

Afterwards they adjourned to the drawing-room for coffee, and Olivia accepted a small brandy, in lieu of a liqueur. It was only as she was enjoying the taste of the fiery liquid on her tongue that she realised she had been a little hasty in taking it. Sherry, wine with the rack of lamb, and now brandy was quite a quantity of alcohol for someone whose head for such things had already proved unreliable, and she was further disconcerted when Lady Lavinia came to join her on the plush green sofa. Like her guest, Matthew's mother was carrying a goblet containing a measure of brandy, but Olivia felt herself stiffening again as the older woman's eyes speared hers.

'So,' she said softly, 'you decided to come back.'

'O-only for the funeral,' murmured Olivia quickly, aware of Matthew sitting at the piano, picking out a tune on the keys. The impressive grand piano was in the window embrasure some distance away, and she wondered if he could hear what his mother was saying. Probably not, she decided, and then changed her mind when he looked up and found her gaze upon him. 'Um— I'm going back to New York in a few days.'

'Are you?' She couldn't tell whether Lady Lavinia was relieved or not. 'You must like living in the United States.'

'Well, it's my home,' said Olivia, wishing her words held more conviction. She looked up at Matthew's father, who was standing beside the flower-filled fireplace. 'It— it was very kind of you to invite me here.'

'After everything that's happened? Yes.' Lady Lavinia didn't dispute the fact, and earned an impatient sigh from her husband. 'But, as I said on the phone, I prefer not to incite gossip. There has been enough talk about this family in recent years——'

'Oh, Mother!'

Matthew broke off his playing then to give his mother an imploring look, but Lady Lavinia merely tilted her head. 'It's true,' she said. 'With Olivia running off like that, causing everyone to think she must be pregnant, and that you'd refused to marry her. And then Helen proving to be so mercenary——'

'I don't think Olivia wants to hear this, Vinnie,' her husband exclaimed wearily, but Lady Lavinia wouldn't be silent.

'Why not?' she demanded. She turned to Olivia. 'Were you pregnant? Was that why you left? If I do have a grandchild somewhere, that I've never been allowed to meet, I'd like to know.'

Olivia felt terrible now. 'There—there was no—baby,' she said, incapable of meeting Matthew's eyes. 'I'm sorry if people thought there was, but it wasn't true. I—I wouldn't have done that to—to anyone.'

Or would she? If she had found out she was pregnant, after what her grandmother had told her, it would have been the only thing to do.

Lady Lavinia's nostrils flared. 'Then it was as Matthew said: you simply didn't want to settle down?'

Olivia expelled an unsteady breath. 'Yes.'

Lady Lavinia shook her head. 'I find that very hard to believe, Olivia.'

'Why?' It was Matthew who spoke now, and Olivia realised he had left the piano to come and stand beside

his father. 'Why should you find it hard to believe,
Mother? You were never entirely in accord with our relationship, were you? Perhaps Olivia felt she couldn't
stand the opposition.'

'Oh, no.' His mother looked up at him now, and her
face was strangely anguished. 'No, I won't have that accusation levelled at me, Matthew. Not again. I may not
always have approved of your association with Olivia,
but I never stopped you from seeing her. Not once. You
can't still blame me for what she did. Dear God, haven't
I suffered——?'

'I think we've all said enough about the past,' broke
in Mr Ryan heavily, and for once his normally good-
humoured features were grave. 'Vinnie, I'm sure Olivia
didn't come here to listen to a catechism about what she
did more than ten years ago. All right, we all felt pretty
bad about it at the time, including Olivia herself, I dare
say. But her reasons are no longer valid. For pity's sake,
let it rest in peace!'

There was silence after this announcement, and Olivia
forgot her misgivings and drank the brandy, because it
gave her something to do. She should never have come
here, she thought. No matter what her father had said,
she should have refused Lady Lavinia's invitation. She
should have known something like this was bound to
happen. The Ryans were only human, after all. And in
their eyes her behaviour must seem inexcusable.

Eventually, Mr Ryan tried to ease the situation by
saying something about the current dry spell to Matthew,
and Matthew responded in kind by telling his father that
one of the old men in the village had assured him that
rain was coming. They had a brief discussion about the
merits of amateur forecasters, and then Olivia put her
empty glass aside, and got determinedly to her feet.

'I think I ought to go,' she said, trying not to sound
as desperate as she felt. 'Er—we keep early hours at
home. Dad has to be up for milking at half-past five.'

'Of course.' Predictably, it was Matthew's father who
answered her, and she was grateful to him for his un-
derstanding. 'I'll—er—I'll run you home myself.'

'That won't be necessary.' Matthew looked at his father now, and they exchanged a telling glance. 'I'll take Olivia home,' he said, and his mother breathed a sigh of relief.

'Thanks.'

Olivia felt obliged to make the expected rejoinder, and then the elder Ryans accompanied them to the door.

'It has been good to see you again, Olivia,' Matthew's father assured her, as Matthew collected a jacket from the cloakroom, and even Lady Lavinia unbent sufficiently to add her endorsement to her husband's.

'Perhaps one day you'll come back and see us again,' she said, and Olivia couldn't tell from her expression whether she meant it or not.

'Perhaps so,' Olivia murmured non-committally, and then Matthew was back, his leather jacket complementing his dark appearance.

'Let's go,' he said briskly, and Olivia made a final apologetic gesture before following him out to the car.

Although it wasn't a cold evening, the air outside was much fresher than it had been indoors, and Olivia immediately felt the effects of the incautious amount of alcohol she had consumed. She wasn't used to mixing her drinks, and it took an amazing amount of determination to reach the car without deviating. She didn't feel drunk, just a little light-headed; but she wished she hadn't accepted the brandy, which had evidently been larger than she thought.

Still, once she was safely inside the car, she relaxed a little. The evening was over, and she had succeeded in handling it with comparative restraint. After all, it wasn't every day she was expected to sit down to supper with a man who didn't know she was his daughter. Or with the man she loved more than life itself, she reflected bitterly, but who was forever denied to her...

CHAPTER TWELVE

'ARE you all right?'

Matthew was speaking to her now, and Olivia turned her head to look at him. His expression was hidden from her, but his profile was achingly familiar, and it took an actual physical effort not to reach out and touch him.

'Um—I'm fine,' she said instead, aware that her breathing was anything but. 'It's—er—it's been a very pleasant evening.'

'Has it?' Matthew uttered a short mirthless laugh. 'I'm glad you think so.'

'Well, hasn't it?' Olivia determined not to let him see how his words had disconcerted her. 'I thought the meal was delicious. That salmon mousse——'

'Cut it out,' said Matthew harshly. 'I'm not talking about the food, and you know it!'

'Do I?'

'You should.' He took his eyes from the road for a moment to give her an unfathomable look. 'If I'd known the old lady was going to bring up all that stuff about you being pregnant when you went away I'd have found some way to block the invitation.'

Olivia quivered. 'I see.' She moistened her lips. 'You—you didn't ever—I mean—you didn't ever think that, did you?'

'That you were pregnant?' Matthew's lips twisted. 'No.'

Olivia never knew why she pursued it, but she did. 'Why not?' she asked curiously, and Matthew sighed.

'Why would you run out on me if you were pregnant?' he demanded impatiently. 'God knows, I wanted to marry you.'

Olivia hesitated. 'But—I didn't want to settle down, did I?' she pointed out provokingly, and with a sound of irritation Matthew stepped on the brakes.

'What are we talking about here?' he grated, turning in his seat to look at her. 'Were you pregnant? Is that what you're saying? Did you run away because you thought I wouldn't let you get rid of it or something?'

'No!' Olivia was wishing she hadn't started this now. It was the brandy talking, she thought unhappily. Running away with her tongue, and her common sense.

'So what are you saying?' Matthew persisted, and Olivia looked about her a little apprehensively, realising they were still on Ryan land. Matthew had stopped a few yards from the gates of the estate, and safety—in the form of the village—was still some significant distance away.

'I'm not saying anything,' she mumbled, a little ruefully. 'I just wondered—what you did think, that's all. It was a foolish thought. Forget it. It doesn't matter now.'

'Of course it matters,' muttered Matthew, and she was aware that his arm was along the back of the seat behind her. 'If I'd thought you were pregnant, I'd have moved heaven and earth to get you back. But I thought there was someone else. It was the only thing that made any sense.'

'Oh.'

Olivia made the word sound final, hoping he would take the hint and start the engine again. But he didn't. The silence stretched between them, taut with unspoken need, and she knew that if she didn't say something soon the unforgivable would happen.

'Was there someone else?'

Matthew's voice was not quite steady, and she was not really surprised when she felt his hand touch her nape, his fingers strong and possessive. She felt an almost overwhelming urge to tip her head back against his hand, and let sensuality overtake her, but she didn't. Even though she wanted to reassure him, to tell him that she had never loved anyone but him, a shred of sanity pre-

vailed. But she wished that she could tell him why. He
deserved to know the truth.

'Olivia?'

His breath invaded her ear, warm and only lightly
scented with the wine he had drunk at supper. She had
noticed that, unlike her, he had been rather conservative
with his drinking—which was why he was not now suffering from the effects of an unstable constitution, she
reflected nervously.

Realising she had to do something to stop him, she
said the first thing that came into her head. 'Helen came
to see me yesterday,' she ventured weakly, and although
Matthew didn't draw back she sensed his wary evalu-
ation of her words.

'Did she?' he said at last, and there was weariness, as
well as enquiry, in his voice. 'I didn't know you'd been
in touch with her, since you came back.'

'I haven't.' Olivia couldn't let him think that, but she
did regret betraying Helen's confidence. 'Uh—I suppose
she wanted to offer her condolences. As she didn't go
to the funeral——'

Matthew swore then, and Olivia, who had been trying
to think of some other way to distract him, suddenly
found her wishes granted. Without any further effort on
her part, she was free, and Matthew was raking his hand
through his hair, with every appearance of frustration.

'Don't give me that!' he said harshly, and Olivia, who
was just recovering from the shock of his withdrawal,
gazed at him helplessly.

'I beg your——'

'I said don't lie to me, Olivia!' he declared savagely.
'Helen didn't go to see you because she felt any sympathy for your grandmother's death. She hardly knew
the woman, and even if she had met her, which I doubt,
she wouldn't care what happened to her. Helen's not
like that. Helen doesn't get involved in what she would
regard as—trivialities. All Helen cares about are her
horses, and she'll do anything—*anything*—to keep
them!'

Olivia swallowed. For a moment there, she had been half afraid he had guessed the real reason for Helen's visit, and while she felt no real sense of loyalty towards the other girl she had believed her when she had said that Matthew would find her attitude humiliating. But, it seemed she still had a chance to divert his suspicions—though how she was to do that, she didn't know.

However, as she was pondering her dilemma, Matthew spoke again.

'Are you going to tell me why she really came to see you?' he asked, resting his arms on the steering-wheel, and turning his head towards her. 'Or shall I tell you?'

Olivia had backed herself into a corner, and she knew it. 'I—don't know what you mean,' she protested, wondering why she kept allowing herself to get into these situations. 'I've told you why she came. She—she was really very nice.'

'*Nice!*' The way Matthew said the word was just the opposite. 'I bet she was bloody nice! Helen can be charming, when you've got something she wants.'

Olivia blinked. 'Something she wants?'

'I just wonder how she found out,' Matthew went on broodingly. 'She knew I went to pick you up from the plane, but that meant nothing. And, as you say, she didn't attend the funeral. Someone has to have said something. Someone who saw us that day in your father's study. My guess is Enid Davis. I doubt if your mother would have spread the word around.'

Olivia's mouth was dry, but she managed to sound confused. 'Matt, what are you——?'

'—talking about?' he finished for her. 'Don't pretend you don't know. I'm talking about us—about our relationship. About the fact that, when I touch you, everyone else ceases to exist.'

'No——'

'Yes.' His hand turned her face towards him. 'That's why Helen came to see you. Because she knows how I feel about you.'

Olivia trembled. 'You mean—you think she's—jealous!'

'No!' It had been a long shot, and she had hardly believed it herself. 'I mean Helen knows you're the only person who might persuade me to ask for a divorce. That's why she came to see you, isn't it? Oh, don't bother to deny it. I can see it in your eyes.'

Olivia sniffed. 'It's too dark to see my eyes.'

'All right. I can feel it through your skin. Call it osmosis; call it having a sixth sense where you're concerned. I don't care. It's the truth, isn't it? Please don't lie again.'

'All right, it's the truth,' said Olivia unsteadily, trying to draw away from him, but he wouldn't let her. His long fingers lay smooth and hard against her cheek, and everywhere they touched, the blood rose hotly to the surface of her skin. 'I—I'm sorry if it embarrasses you, but she did ask me not to tell you——'

'I bet she did.'

'—and—and I've betrayed her confidence. You don't understand, Matt, she was only thinking of you——'

'Like hell!' Matthew's response was violent. 'I've told you, the only thing Helen cares about are her precious horses. And right now they're in jeopardy.'

Olivia was confused. 'I don't think I——'

'Liv, she wants me to ask her for a divorce. Can't you see that? It's the only way she can ensure the continuation of the Berrenger Stables!'

Olivia stared at him. 'Why?'

'Why do you think? She needs money. Lots of money. And God help me! I can't give her any more. Not without selling the farms.'

Olivia tried to absorb what he was saying. 'But she said—— '

'Yes? What did she say?'

'That—that she's asked you for a divorce.'

'And will you believe me if I tell you she hasn't?'

Olivia shook her head. 'I don't know what to believe.'

'Then let me lay it on the line for you, shall I?'
Matthew withdrew his hand and hunched down in his
seat. 'When Helen's father died, the stables were losing
money. They were mortgaged to the hilt and without the
insurance Conrad had taken out on his own life they'd
have had to be sold.'

Olivia nodded. 'Helen—Helen said something like
that.'

'OK.' Matthew considered his words for a moment,
and then went on, 'So—after her father died, we got
married. Did she tell you about that?'

'She said—she said you had married her on the
rebound.'

Matthew snorted. 'Decent of her.' He paused. 'Yes,
well, I guess that is the kindest way to put it. I didn't
much care what happened to me after you went away,
and my father and Conrad Berrenger had been friends
for years.'

Olivia bent her head. 'So—you got married,' she said,
hurrying him on. She didn't want to think about that
marriage, however expedient it might have been.

'Yes.' Matthew struck the wheel with the flat of his
hand. 'And Helen got her money.'

'So—so everything was all right.'

'No, it wasn't.' Matthew sighed. 'What I didn't know
at that time was that my father had been subsidising
Conrad for years, that he had mortgaged Rycroft in a
last-ditch attempt to help his friend, and that when
Conrad died he didn't get a penny of the insurance
money.'

'So—so that's why——'

'—we're broke?' Matthew tone was sardonic. 'You
could say that.'

Olivia was appalled. 'But—couldn't the stables have
been sold?'

'They could have been, if my father had been willing
to turn Helen out. But you know him. He's not that
kind of man. And God knows, he suffered when Conrad
took his own life.'

'But he'd done all he could.'

'I know.' Matthew expelled his breath wearily. 'But it wasn't enough in his eyes, and since then he's done everything he can to keep the stables going.'

'Including selling some of Rycroft land?'

'Even that. Though not the farms, so far.'

Including *her* father's farm, though Olivia, with dismay. What would her father do if he lost his livelihood? Not to mention Andrew, and his young family...

'Oh, don't worry.' Matthew seemed to sense her anxiety. 'He won't sell your father's farm. Not if I can help it. Indeed, lately, I think I've managed to persuade him that there's nothing more he can do. And I guess that's why Helen got this idea of approaching you. Your return couldn't have been more opportune as far as she's concerned.'

'But why should she think——?'

'*Liv!*' Matthew turned his head and looked at her, his eyes hooded and intent. 'She knows—has always known—that you're the only person who could persuade me to ask for a divorce!'

'Even so——'

'Liv, she'd do it for a price. Do you understand? A nice friendly divorce, for a fee. Payment on demand. No questions asked.'

Olivia frowned. 'But—you could get a divorce anyway. You don't live together, do you?'

'Can you prove that?' Matthew's tone was laconic. 'The first hint that I might be divorcing her, and Helen would be back at Rycroft immediately. And do you think my father would stop her? Not a chance.'

'But—you could leave Rycroft.'

'And leave my father to Helen's machinations? No way. Where divorce is concerned, she's got me over a barrel, and she knows it. Your coming back was just an added bonus.'

'Why?' Olivia was bewildered, and Matthew groaned.

'Why do you think? Why are we sitting here now, talking about it? Because we both know we don't want the evening to end.'

'No——'

'Yes,' he cut in angrily, but he didn't touch her. 'That's what makes this whole situation so bloody.'

'No.' Olivia drew back into the corner of the seat. 'Matt—you're wrong——'

'Am I?' He stared at her in the darkness, and she could feel the heat of his eyes. 'If I touched you now, would you stop me? Did you stop me on the day of your grand-mother's funeral?'

'That was different?'

'How was it different?'

'I'd been drinking.'

'You've been drinking tonight.'

'Matt, stop this!' Olivia drew a labouring breath. 'It's useless, and you know it. I—I didn't come back because of you. I came back because my mother asked me to.'

'You wouldn't have come back if I had asked you to?'

'No.' She gulped as his hand closed over her knee. *'No!'*

'Do you want me to prove you wrong?' he demanded harshly, leaning towards her, and suddenly there was no air in the car.

'I'm—I'm going to marry—Perry,' she got out chokingly, scrabbling for the handle of the door. 'Please, Matt, let me out of here. I don't think I can take any more.'

Matthew slumped in his seat, and the electric window glided down beside her. 'Calm down,' he said, leaning forward and flicking the ignition switch. 'You don't have to panic. I'll take you home. Your father would never forgive me if I didn't.'

But he's not my father; yours is, Olivia wanted to scream, her emotions swept to fever pitch by the agony of the situation. And if her mother had never got involved with his father Helen wouldn't have this hold on him now.

But commonsense prevailed, and by the time they reached the farm Olivia was able to thank him for bringing her home, and ask him if he'd like to come in for a nightcap. There were lights still glowing through the drawing-room curtains, and she guessed her parents would expect Matthew to show his face.

But for once Matthew declined, and in the illumination cast by his headlights she saw his gaunt expression. It tore her heart, and she knew it would take the utmost determination on her part to get out of the car without saying something to reassure him. She knew what she wanted to say—that she loved him, and that she'd live with him forever, if she could, with or without the sanction of a wedding-ring. She didn't care about Helen, or the Berrenger stables; she didn't even care about Rycroft, except in so far as it affected all their lives. She only cared about Matthew. And she wanted him to know that.

He looked at her then, and something of what she was feeling evidently showed in her face, for he made a strangled sound, and moved towards her. Before she could even think of stopping him, his hand was at the back of her neck, tipping her face up to his. And when his mouth touched hers, her lips parted automatically.

It was heaven to be this close to him again, and she thought fleetingly of those occasions in the past when he had brought her home, and they had spent long satisfying minutes sitting in his Mini, saying goodnight. He had kissed her then, too, though not so urgently, and his tongue in her mouth had never felt so desperate. It was as if he knew, as she did, that this was the last chance they would ever have to be alone together, and her senses swam beneath the dark passion of his demands.

'God, Liv, don't—don't leave me,' he groaned, against her neck, and her hand slipped into the open collar of his shirt to pull him closer.

And then, light spilled out of the opened door of the farm house, dazzling in its brilliance, and Matthew swore

as Olivia jerked away from him. But even he recognised
the incongruity of her father's witnessing their embrace,
and, thrusting open his door, he got out of the car.

'Bob,' he said politely, and only Olivia heard the strain
in his voice. But even as she was silently congratulating
Matthew for his control, another man appeared behind
her father, and her stomach plunged when she realised
his identity. It was Perry, slim and elegant, in his pale
grey trousers and matching shirt, a silk cravat filling the
opening of his collar.

'Oh, God!' she breathed inaudibly, and although it
was the last thing she wanted to do she, too, pushed
open her door and got out of the car.

'You've got a visitor, Livvy,' her father greeted her,
but she could tell his reaction to Perry's arrival was only
marginally more enthusiastic than Matthew's.

As for Matthew himself, he suffered Robert Stoner's
introduction with unsmiling civility. But, as it happened, Perry had seen Olivia, and any inadequacies on
Matthew's part were overlooked in his delight at seeing
her.

'Darling,' he exclaimed, launching himself at her, and
Olivia had no choice but to let him take her in his arms
and kiss her.

As a kiss, Perry's salutation left much to be desired,
but Olivia knew that no small part of its deficiency was
due to her. She could hardly bear to let him touch her,
and her eyes stayed open, observing Matthew's response
with an aching sense of loss.

But apparently there were limits to what even Matthew
was prepared to stand, and, refusing Robert Stoner's
offer of refreshment, he walked back to his car.

'Goodnight,' he said stiffly, including them all in one
sweeping glance, and Olivia had to stand, with Perry's
arm about her, as Matthew drove away.

CHAPTER THIRTEEN

Two days later, Olivia sat on the bed in her grand-mother's bedroom, watching her mother sift through the contents of her grandmother's wardrobe. Although she hadn't welcomed the task of helping her mother sort out her grandmother's things, it did give her an excuse for leaving Perry to his own devices, and in the last two days she had had few opportunities to do so. As soon as she came downstairs in the morning he was there, and al-though she appreciated the fact that his only reason for coming here was to find her and take her back to the United States with him, she wished he were less de-manding in his attitude. She had told him she would leave with him at the end of the week, and she would. But until then she needed some space and he wasn't giving her any.

The truth was, of course, she wished he hadn't come here. It was stupid, perhaps, particularly as she was expected to marry him as soon as they returned to New York, but Perry didn't belong here. It wasn't anything he did particularly; he had been excessively polite to both her parents and, although her father evidently found him a little strange in his habits, even he had had to accept that the man was sincere. But, in all honesty, she didn't want him here, and, if she examined her reasons why, she would have to say that it was because his arrival had prevented her from seeing Matthew again.

And that shouldn't have been a bad thing, she thought despairingly, smoothing the worn bedspread beneath her fingers. For God's sake, after the way she had behaved the other night, she ought to be glad that Perry's presence had had the involuntary effect of preventing her from making matters worse. For that was what would have happened, she was sure of it. Where Matthew was concerned, her resistance was losing its conviction, and there were times when she didn't know which was worse—his unhappiness or her own torment.

'Oh, I think all these things can go to the church jumble sale,' said her mother suddenly, pulling an armful of woollies out of the wardrobe, and tossing them on to the bed. 'I know the vicar's wife will appreciate them, and I'm sure it's what your grandmother would have wanted. Don't you agree?'

'What?' Olivia had been lost in thought, and only the sight of the woollens on the bed gave her some indication of what her mother had been asking. 'Oh—um— yes,' she answered, not really knowing what she was agreeing to, and her mother regarded her with resignation.

'What's the matter, Livvy?' she asked. 'I'm getting quite worried about you. I thought you'd be pleased that Mr Randall is here, but you're not, are you?'

'His name's Perry,' said Olivia, without answering her question, and Mrs Stoner's lips drew in as she recognised the diversion.

'I prefer to call him *Mr* Randall,' she declared. 'We hardly know him, Livvy. He's your friend, not ours. If— and you've not really told us what your plans are, so far as he is concerned—if you do intend to marry the man, then naturally we'll be obliged to accept him as a member of the family, but until then——'

Olivia sighed. 'You don't like him, do you?'

'I didn't say that.' Her mother shook her head. 'We hardly know him, as I say——'

'But you don't like what you do know?'

'No. I mean, yes. That's not what I'm saying.' Mrs Stoner looked a little exasperatedly at her daughter now. 'Livvy, we're just not used to his ways, that's all. I mean—eating yoghurt for breakfast! What's wrong with good old-fashioned toast and marmalade?'

Olivia had to laugh, in spite of herself. 'There's nothing wrong with toast and marmalade,' she said. 'But we generally eat white bread, and Perry doesn't. Plus the fact that the marmalade you make is full of sugar.'

'Oh, well——' Mrs Stoner made an expressive gesture, and turned back to the wardrobe. 'It doesn't appear to have harmed your father, and young Sara's husband says it's the best he's tasted.'

'It is.' Olivia lifted her shoulders. 'It's just Perry's way. His diet's very important to him.'

'Well, I've always thought that when you're a guest in someone's house, you should be prepared to compromise,' retorted her mother, rummaging about in the bottom of the cupboard. 'Which reminds me, Mrs Davis says that he's asked for his sheets to be changed every day. Does he do that at home?'

'I believe so.' Olivia shrugged. 'So, you don't like him?'

'I'm not—enamoured of him, no.' Mrs Stoner pulled a face. 'But that's not to say there's anything wrong with him.' She sighed. 'You're the one who has to decide if he's the man for you. Not your father or me.'

'But, if I did marry him——'

'—you'd both be welcome here, and you know it,' cut in her mother crisply. 'Just as Sara and her husband always are. And that's another thing: I haven't heard from Sara since she went back. I hope she's all right. That baby's very near its time.'

Olivia hesitated. She would have liked to ask her mother who she thought the man for her should be, but she didn't. It was always like this. Whenever the opportunity to pursue the truth presented itself, she always drew back. How could she accuse her mother of lying to her—to her husband—all these years? Another heart attack could be fatal, and Olivia couldn't have that burden on her conscience.

So, instead, she said tautly, 'Your first grandchild. You must be very excited.'

'Oh, yes.' Mrs Stoner had unearthed what appeared to be a deed box in the bottom of the wardrobe, and she indicated that Olivia should come and lift it out for her. 'And poor Sara's having to carry the baby to full term. I didn't have that problem with any of mine.'

Olivia paused in the process of lifting the deed box on to her mother's lap. 'You didn't?' she asked faintly.

'No.' Felicity Stoner took the box from her unresisting fingers, and set it on her knee. 'For some reason, all my babies were born at seven or eight months. You were the earliest, I remember. Barely seven months after your father and I got married.'

Olivia swallowed, and sat down on the bed again rather heavily. 'Really?' she said, her face suffusing with colour for no apparent reason. 'How—how unusual.'

'Yes, it was.' Happily, her mother was intent on opening the deed box and didn't notice her daughter's embarrassment. 'But some women are like that. The doctor said it was perfectly natural.'

Olivia absorbed this with some difficulty. How could her mother sit there and pretend *she* had been a seven-months baby? According to her grandmother's reckoning, Felicity had been at least two months pregnant when she'd married Robert Stoner. However early her other babies had been, Olivia hadn't been one of them.

The deed box was open now, and Olivia, sitting on the bed beside her mother's wheelchair, felt her eyes drawn to its contents. There was a copy of her grandmother's will, some old photographs, sepia-tinted, as they used to be, and several old pension books, dog-eared with age.

There was also a bundle of letters, bound together with an elastic band, and Olivia watched, with some dismay, as her mother snapped them free.

'My God!' she exclaimed, and Olivia was alarmed at the tremor in her voice. But when she looked into her mother's face there was only anger in her expression. Evidently she had not known that Harriet Stoner had found the letters Matthew's father had written her, and she was reacting to that discovery and nothing else.

'Um—what's wrong?' Olivia asked innocently, sitting on her hands to prevent herself from snatching the letters out of her mother's grasp.

'These,' said Felicity Stoner bitterly, flicking through the envelopes that her daughter had once opened with such dread. 'They're the letters Matt Ryan wrote to me, all those years ago. Your grandmother must have taken them, and kept them for some reason.'

Olivia drew a careful breath. 'Didn't—didn't you keep them?' she asked, trying to sound casual, but her mother shook her head.

'No. Years ago—just after your father and I were married, actually—I threw them all away. I don't know why I kept them that long, really. Except that they had sentimental value, I suppose. They reminded me of my youth.'

Olivia frowned. 'Your youth? But you were only young when you got married.'

'I was twenty-four,' said Felicity ruefully. 'That was old in those days. Particularly in a village like Lower Mychett. After all, your father and I had known one another since our schooldays.'

Olivia licked her lips. 'So—why did you wait so long?' she ventured, wondering if at last her mother was going to tell her the truth, and Mrs Stoner sighed.

'I suppose—because of Matt,' she admitted slowly, opening one of the letters, and briefly scanning its contents. 'You've heard the gossip, I know. But Matt and I did care for one another, however bad that sounds.'

'Bad?' Olivia's voice was hoarse.

'Of course.' Her mother looked up. 'He was married, Livvy. And that, too, meant a lot more in those days. Divorce wasn't easy; not for anyone. And I was just a teenager, not even sure it was what I wanted.'

'A teenager!'

Olivia couldn't help the way her voice rose as she said the words, but her mother was too absorbed with what she was saying to pay much attention to her daughter's reaction.

'Yes. Nineteen,' Mrs Stoner said reminiscently, and Olivia's jaw sagged. 'And Matt was thirty-seven; almost twice my age.'

Olivia could feel the beads of sweat standing out on her forehead, but she had to pursue this now. She had to know if what her grandmother had told her ten years ago was a lie. She had to know if—oh, God!—if Matthew wasn't her brother.

'So—what happened?' she asked, hoping she sounded like any daughter would, faced with her mother's indiscretions. And Felicity lifted her head to stare into space.

'Do you really want to know?' she asked, and Olivia quelled her burning impatience to admit to being curious. *Curious! Dear God.* She dug her nails into the coverlet. She wasn't just curious, she was desperate!

'Well,' said Felicity softly, 'Matt didn't get a divorce, as you know. Which was all for the best, in the circumstances.'

'Wh—what circumstances?'

'Oh——' Her mother turned to give her a doubtful look, and then lifted her thin shoulders. 'Lavinia found she was expecting a baby, you see. After all those years, she chose that time to prove that she and Matt were still sleeping together.'

Olivia's breath caught in her throat. 'I see.'

'Do you?' Felicity arched her brows. 'I wonder.'

'What do you mean?'

Felicity hesitated. 'I was pregnant, too.'

Olivia couldn't speak now. She just stared at her mother in disbelief, and Felicity, misinterpreting her silence, gave a rueful shake of her head. 'I know,' she said. 'You're shocked. I would be, too, if it was my mother telling me these things, but I think you're old enough now to understand that we can't always control our feelings. And—I was young, as I say. And Matt was just like his son—a very attractive man.'

Olivia could feel the hysteria rising in her throat, but she fought it back. 'So—so what did you do?' she asked,

in a voice that didn't sound anything like her own, and
her mother bent her head.

'I didn't have to *do* anything. I miscarried at three
months, so the problem didn't arise. As to what I would
have done, well—I suppose I could have gone away to
have the baby, and then had it adopted. That was also
what young women did in those days. Being a single
mother wasn't the accepted thing it is today.'

'And—and Mr Ryan?'

'Oh, Matt never knew. I did compose a letter once,
but it was never sent. I wanted to tell him, you see. Fool-
ishly, I suppose. But he'd always wanted children, and
it looked as though he and Lavinia couldn't have any.
Then, as I say, Lavinia found she was expecting Matthew,
and I miscarried——'

Olivia was trembling now, and she was glad she was
sitting on her hands so her mother wouldn't notice. 'So—
you told no one.'

'Only your father,' said Mrs Stoner gently. 'I told him
before we got married. I wasn't a virgin, you see. And,
that too, was of some significance then. But—he loved
me enough to forgive me, and that's all that mattered.
Not that your grandmother would have forgiven me, if
she'd known. But happily these letters are from Matt to
me, so she'd have found out nothing damning from
them.'

Except that they're not all from Matthew Ryan to you,
thought Olivia weakly, realising that her mother mustn't
ever find out what Harriet Stoner had done. At present,
Felicity was annoyed, and a little disturbed, that the old
woman had hung on to the letters all these years. If she
must ponder her reasons for doing so, let the doubts still
remain.

'Would—would you like me to destroy them?' Olivia
suggested now, and for the first time her mother noticed
her discomfort.

'You're shivering, Livvy,' she said. 'Are you cold?'

'Just—just a bit,' murmured Olivia, not altogether truthfully. Although the colour had receded from her face, her racing pulse defied moderation.

'I suppose you're surprised now that I encouraged your relationship with Matt's son, aren't you?' her mother asked, misinterpreting her expression. 'But I don't bear him any malice, you know. Matt loved me. I know he did. And nothing would have made us happier than if his son and my daughter had fallen in love.' She shrugged. 'But it wasn't to be. Though for quite a time we thought it was.'

Olivia wanted to weep; but that would come later. Right now, she had to protect her mother. 'Um—shall I burn the letters?' she suggested, keeping her voice light. 'I—don't think—Dad—would appreciate Gran's motives for keeping them either.'

'No. No, you're right.' Her mother nodded, and without examining them any further she thrust them into her daughter's hand. 'Yes. Get rid of them, Livvy. I don't think we should mention them at all. It can be our secret.'

Our secret!

As she lay in bed that night, those words repeated themselves over and over in Olivia's brain, until she thought she would go mad. Our secret! But not her secret, or her grandmother's secret, but her mother's secret. A secret that had been history before she had ever been born.

All these years, she had been believing a lie. Or, if not a lie, then at least a misunderstanding. A *misunderstanding*! Dear God, if only she had had a little more faith in her mother and gone to her when her grandmother had first told her about the letters. If only she had been more trusting, the last ten years could have been *so* different.

And yet, the fact remained that even now she was unable to tell her mother what had happened. And besides, what if it had been true? What if her grandmother's suspicions had been correct? She might have

precipitated the kind of argument that could have only
ended in disaster. And if her father had had no
knowledge of the affair, how might *he* have reacted to
her revelations? Not to mention her mother herself...

No, on reflection, her behaviour was justifiable, even
if it didn't alter the mess she had made of her life. Before
finally destroying the letters, she had read the letter her
mother had written, and never sent, to Matthew Ryan,
one last time, and it was amazing how things leapt out
at her, now that she was seeing it in a different light.
The bit where her mother had said she had wanted to
tell him about the baby, because it was what he had
always wanted, for instance. If she had thought about
that seriously, she might have wondered at the wording.
After all, she had assumed the letter had been written
after Matthew was born, so why would her mother use
those words? And Matthew, too. He wasn't mentioned
at all. Surely her mother would have mentioned him, in
the same way that she had mentioned Lady Lavinia. But
she hadn't. Because he wasn't around. Because he hadn't
even been born!

Of course, it was easy now to see the discrepancies.
Everything was easier with hindsight. And she couldn't
help wondering if her grandmother really had believed
what she had told her. Harriet Stoner had been very
astute, too astute, surely, to be taken in by a mistake.
Yet, if she had known the true story, why had she done
it? There seemed no sense in destroying Olivia's life for
no apparent reason.

Olivia slept badly, and was up at first light, leaning
on the window sill, breathing in the cool country air.
There was nothing like the smell of the country, she
thought. And to someone who had spent the last ten
years in the city, it was doubly appealing.

She doubted Perry would agree with her. He turned
up his nose at country smells, and country ways, and
she knew he was happiest in the air-conditioned luxury
of his New York apartment. Although he insisted on
eating natural foods, he had no real desire to know where

they had come from. His housekeeper did his shopping in the most exclusive health stores available.

Which made his trip to Lower Mychett so uncharacteristic. He had evidently been concerned about her, and she appreciated it. But she had the guilty feeling she was going to disappoint him, as she had once disappointed Matthew. Because she knew she couldn't marry him now. If nothing else, the past twenty-four hours had convinced her of that. So long as she and Matthew were not related, there was always a chance that one day they might come together. Though when that was likely to be was much less easy to hazard.

For, in the dark reaches of the night, after the euphoria of learning that Matthew was not her brother had died down, common sense had reasserted itself. She knew it was all very well thinking how wonderful it was that the emotions she had for Matthew need no longer be denied, to herself at least, but basically the situation as it was now hadn't changed. Oh, she could stop feeling bad for loving him, that was true; but he was still married to Helen, and that was unlikely to be altered. What had Matthew said? That Helen would give him a divorce for a price. But would that price mean her father's livelihood? And if it did, how could she jeopardise his future?

In one respect, at least, she suspected Helen might be right. If—and it was only a hypothetical if—if she were to ask Matthew to divorce Helen and marry her, he might do it, whatever the cost. She had some idea now of how Matthew had suffered when she went away, and, although she might not deserve it, given an ultimatum, he might be prepared to do it.

But she couldn't risk that. Indeed, as the night had worn on, she had come to the awful conclusion that she and Matthew would never have a future together. After all, Helen needed money. That much was obvious. And, without the incentive of some reward for her cooperation, she wasn't going to make it easy for them. There seemed no way Matthew could free himself without disabling the estate completely.

That was why Olivia was up at dawn, knowing it was probably the last time she would spend the night in Lower Mychett. She was going back to New York. She had decided that in the wee small hours. And if she left now, she knew she would never come back. Whatever happened, Matthew would never understand, never forgive her...

CHAPTER FOURTEEN

THE phone rang, and Agnes Reina picked it up. 'It's Perry,' she said, pressing the button that cut her voice off from the caller. 'Do you want to speak to him?'

Olivia sighed, and shook her head. 'No,' she said quickly, and then, as her conscience pricked her, she held out her hand for the receiver. 'Oh—all right. Give it to me. I suppose you can't go on saying I'm in a meeting. But I wish he wouldn't keep calling me.'

Agnes shrugged her slim shoulders. She was a tall, dark, attractive woman, in her mid-thirties, whose part-Asian ancestry was only evident in the olive-tinged smoothness of her skin. She and Olivia had known one another for almost eight years, and for the past seven they had shared the running of the child-nursing agency. With one failed marriage behind her, and a distinct aversion to trying another, Agnes had proved a good friend to the English girl, and she was the only person, outside of Olivia's own family, who knew why she had come to the United States in the first place.

'Why don't you tell him there's someone else?' Agnes suggested now, returning to the pile of applications she had been vetting before the phone rang. 'I find that's a sure-fire put-off.'

'But how can I?' protested Olivia, without releasing the button. 'He'd know that wasn't true.'

'Then make it true,' retorted Agnes flatly. 'You know Glenn Forrester would jump at the chance to——'

'But that would only complicate the situation even more,' exclaimed Olivia unhappily. The young lawyer in the office down the hall had made several attempts to date her, but although she liked him she had no more

desire to get involved with him than she had to continue
her association with Perry.

'Then it's up to you,' said Agnes, washing her hands
of the whole problem. 'By the way, did you get around
to ringing Gillian Stevens? I interviewed her while you
were away, as I said, and I really think you'll be impressed with her credentials.'

Olivia propped her head on one hand. 'No,' she said
now. 'No, I didn't ring her. I forgot, I'm afraid. Just
give me a minute to deal with this, and I'll get round to
it.' Her head was aching, as she released the hold button.
'Hello, Perry. Can I help you?'

'You can start answering my calls yourself,' Perry retorted testily, and she heaved a heavy sigh.

'I'm sorry——'

'So you should be. Do you realise I've not seen you
once since we got back?'

Olivia shook her head. 'I have been busy,
Perry——'

'Not that busy. I've called your apartment a dozen
times, and all I get is your answering machine.'

Olivia felt guilty. She had left the answerphone on
deliberately. It wasn't that she had been out. Only when
she got home in the evenings she was usually too weary
to take any more calls.

'What can I say?' she murmured now, and Agnes
looked up from her desk to give her a resigned look.

'You can say you'll have dinner with me tonight,' Perry
declared forcefully. 'I think you owe it to me, Olivia. If
this is the brush-off, at least have the guts to tell me so
in person.'

'All right.'

Olivia gave in, and as if unable to believe in her un-
qualified submission Perry added, 'All right—what?'
rather warily.

'All right. I'll have dinner with you,' said Olivia
equably, ignoring Agnes's knowing shake of her head.
'Um—call for me at seven-thirty, will you? I may be late
home, and I'll need some time to shower and change.'

'OK.'

Perry sounded as surprised as he obviously felt, but Olivia replaced her receiver with the air of someone who had achieved a minor victory. 'Well,' she said, before Agnes could make any biting comment, 'I do owe it to him, to be honest. Tonight, I'll tell him I can't see him again. I should have done it weeks ago.'

'Really?'

Agnes didn't sound convinced, and Olivia couldn't altogether blame her. It was three weeks since she had returned from England, and since then she had been making excuses for not seeing Perry. She knew why, of course. They had been friends for a lot of years, and she had depended upon him in the past. Seeing Matthew again had weakened her, she realised that now. Without his influence, she wouldn't be finding her independence so daunting, or putting off making the final break with Perry. But the truth was, for the first time in her life, she was afraid of facing the future alone.

Still, she had no right to use Perry as she had been doing, and that was why she was going to do what she should have done when she first got back from England. She hoped he would understand. He had been a good friend, and she didn't like hurting him. But, whatever happened, he had to know she couldn't marry him. Not now. Not ever.

In the event, Olivia arrived home earlier than she had anticipated. In a fit of generosity, Agnes had suggested she take the rest of the afternoon off to prepare for the evening. 'You look tired,' she said frankly, and Olivia pulled a wry face. 'Have a rest,' she added. 'You look as though you need it. And stop worrying. Everything will turn out for the best. You'll see.'

Olivia wished she could believe her. As she shed her shoes and jacket in the foyer of her apartment, she could see no glimmer of light in the dark tunnel of her days, no shred of hope in the fabric of her despair.

She *would* get over it. She told herself that. She had got over Matthew before, and she would do it again. Or so she hoped. The trouble was, she was older now, and she felt everything much more strongly. And now she knew that time didn't heal all wounds. Some were simply too deep to heal. And she had the feeling that even the catharsis of leaving England, of putting more than three thousand miles between them, was not going to help her this time.

Leaving England had not proved to be a problem, she recalled, treading heavily into her sunlit living-room. Oh, her parents—and she could really think of both of them as her parents now—had been sorry to see her go, but they thought she loved Perry, and she hadn't disillusioned them. It was easier that way. If she had even intimated that anything else was the case, she would have been bogged down with explanations—explanations she didn't want to give. For how could she explain why she had left home ten years ago, if she admitted now that she loved Matthew? Besides, even if she could have got over that obstacle, there was still Helen to think of, and, whatever Matthew said, she was his wife.

Still, it had been quite a relief not to see Matthew again before she left. Given what she now knew, would she have been strong enough to tell him goodbye, or would the inherent weakness she had where he was concerned have overwhelmed her? Happily, she had not had to put it to the test, and she and Perry had left without hindrance, the day after that disturbing conversation with her mother.

Now, Olivia padded into her bedroom, dropping her shoes in the bottom of her wardrobe and taking off the rest of her clothes before going into the adjoining bathroom. She was hot, and tired, as Agnes had said, and after a shower she was going to take her friend's advice and have a rest. She would need all her strength to face Perry this evening.

Actually, she did fall asleep, for a short time at least, and when she awakened she did feel a little more re freshed. Sufficiently so to take the time to choose something attractive from her wardrobe, so that when Perry rang her bell she knew she was looking her best.

She opened the door at once, the folds of her amethyst-coloured silk georgette culotte suit swinging about her slim legs. With her hair loose, and silky-soft about her shoulders, she looked young and appealing, and only the dusky shadows beneath her eyes betrayed her inner conflict.

'At last,' remarked Perry tersely, stepping forward, so that she was obliged to move aside to let him into the apartment. 'I was beginning to think I'd offended you.'

'Offended me?' Olivia used his words to give herself time to think of a reply. 'No. Why should you think that? I told you, I've been busy, that's all.'

'Have you?'

Perry paused in the middle of her living-room and folded his arms, and Olivia wondered if, when they first met, she had not been subconsciously looking for someone who was the exact opposite of Matthew. Perry was fairly tall, it was true, but that was the only resemblance between them. Where Matthew was broad-shouldered and muscular, Perry was slim and slightly effete, and although his hair was expertly tinted these days he had always been fair. Fair-skinned, and fair-minded, she hoped, dreading having to tell him that she couldn't see him again.

'Well—not precisely,' she admitted now. 'Perry, there's something I have to tell you——'

'Surprise me,' he remarked, shaking his head. 'Doesn't the condemned man even get a drink before the axe falls?'

Olivia's face flooded with colour. 'I—don't know what you mean.'

'Oh, don't give me that, Olivia, please.' Perry regarded her with asperity. 'I'd have to be particularly wooden not to know that you've been avoiding me since we came back from England. I assumed there was someone else. So why don't you put me out of my misery?'

'Oh, Perry.' Conversely, Olivia felt awful now, and crossing to the liquor cabinet, she poured him the gimlet she knew he preferred. 'I'm going to miss you.'

'Are you?' Perry came to take the drink from her, and sipped it thoughtfully. Then, finding it to his liking, he added, 'Does it have to be like that?'

Olivia looked puzzled. 'Like what?'

'Us. Not seeing one another,' explained Perry, looking at her over the rim of his glass. 'I'd like to think we could still be—friends.'

Olivia blinked. 'You would?'

'Why not? You might just get tired of this new man, whoever he is. And I'd like to be around to pick up the pieces.'

'Oh.' Olivia shook her head now. 'I'm not seeing anyone else.'

Perry put his drink down and stared at her. 'You're not serious!'

Olivia swallowed. 'I am.'

Perry was amazed. 'But then why——?'

'It's a long story,' said Olivia, turning away from him, and putting some distance between them. She crossed her arms across her body, and gripped her elbows. 'There is someone; someone in England. But—he's married, and—he can't get a divorce.'

'The man you ran away from in the first place?' suggested Perry shrewdly, and she cast him a startled look over her shoulder before deciding there was no point in prevaricating, and nodded her head. 'I see.'

There was silence for a while, as Perry retrieved his drink and savoured the sharp flavour of the gin, and Olivia did her best to recover her composure. It had been quite a shock to realise she was so transparent, though she was grateful not to have to labour her point. Still, Perry's attitude had made her feel better, and when she turned and found him looking at her she only hesitated a moment before going to him.

'You know,' she said, reaching up to bestow a warm kiss on his cheek, 'you really are one of the nicest men I've ever——'

And it was as her lips touched Perry's dry skin that she saw Matthew. He was standing, motionless, in the doorway that led from the foyer of the apartment, and she realised, belatedly, that she hadn't locked the door. But even so, the doorman downstairs would not have let anyone come up unannounced unless she had warned him she was expecting them. So, although instinct caused her to draw back from Perry, her common sense told her she had to be hallucinating. Matthew couldn't be here; not in New York; not in her apartment. What she was seeing was a figment of her imagination, and it was her imagination that was painting that savage expression on his face. His image was the one she most wanted to see, and his anger was her way of justifying his presence.

Even so, his image was so real, she couldn't help but respond to it. She actually felt the guilt she would have felt had Matthew found her in this situation. Putting up a hand to her head, she felt the perspiration beading on her forehead, and she swayed a little unsteadily as the colour drained from her face.

Perry, ever vigilant of her feelings, gazed at her with some concern. 'My dear,' he exclaimed. 'What's wrong. You look as if you've just seen a ghost!'

'Not a ghost, I'm afraid,' remarked Matthew flatly, stepping reluctantly into the room. 'Just the skeleton at the feast.'

And Olivia fainted.

It was daylight when she opened her eyes; *still* daylight, she amended, as with an aching head she pushed herself up against the pillows. But not just any pillows, she realised, recognising the bedspread, but her pillows, the pillows on her bed, where someone must have deposited her, after she lost consciousness. But *who*?

The sickening recollection of what had happened swept over her. But even now she wasn't precisely sure what

was real and what wasn't. She had seen Matthew. She
remembered that. But whether he had actually been here
or she had simply conjured him up was part of the
nightmare. She remembered Perry asking her if she was
all right. She remembered feeling ill. But whether
Matthew had actually said what she thought he said,
before the floor came up and hit her, was something she
had yet to deal with.

A shadow moved against the half-drawn blinds at the
window, and she jerked her head round to see what it
was. The action caused her head to throb, but she ignored the discomfort. A man was standing with his back
to the light, and it took all her concentration to guess
his identity.

'P-Perry?' she whispered faintly, even though the size
and bulk of the man belied her tremulous assumption.
But, even now, she found it difficult to believe that
Matthew might be here, particularly as she remembered
how angry he had looked.

'He's gone,' the man said, moving towards the bed,
and she caught her breath at the realisation that it really
was Matthew. He had shed the jacket he had been
wearing when she'd first seen him in the foyer of the
apartment, and his hands were tucked into the pockets
of his grey trousers. A cream silk shirt completed his
outfit, at present unfastened at the neck, the cuffs turned
back over his forearms. He looked cool, and casual, but
also excessively weary, the lines around his eyes an indication of his exhaustion.

'Gone?' Olivia said now, as he halted beside the bed,
his knees brushing the silk coverlet. It was the only thing
she could think of to say, and Matthew inclined his head,
before turning to sit down beside her.

'Gone,' he agreed, without taking his hands out of
his pockets, giving her an intense appraisal. 'So? How
are you feeling? It's the first time I've had that effect
on a woman.'

She realised he was trying to lighten the situation, but
she couldn't respond. 'Where—where has Perry gone?'

she persisted, remembering the savage look on Matthew's face when he had seen them together. What had happened after she 'dropped out' of the situation? What had they said to one another. Oh, God, she hoped there had been no violence. There was no evidence in Matthew's features, but he was a much stronger man.

'Home, I guess,' Matthew was saying now, taking one hand out of his pocket, and smoothing his palm against the coverlet. 'Or out to dinner. That was where he was planning to take you, wasn't it? I'm sorry if you wanted to join him. But he understood that we have to talk.'

'Did he?' Olivia looked at him with wide anxious eyes. 'Did he understand? Wh-what did you say to him, Matthew? How—how did you persuade him to go?'

'Well, I didn't chuck him out of the window, if that's what you're afraid of,' responded Matthew drily. 'Although, I must admit, when I got here I wanted to. But—old Perry and I—we had an—illuminating conversation. I guess you could say we understand one another now. Which is more than you and I ever did.'

Olivia blinked, and pushed herself further up the bed. She was still wearing the georgette culotte suit, and the wide legs of the trousers caught against the silk, and exposed a tempting length of thigh as she wriggled back. But she managed to push them down again, avoiding Matthew's eyes as she did so. In spite of what he had said, she still had a feeling of unreality in all this, and she wondered if she was still unconscious, and dreaming the whole thing.

'Are you all right?' Matthew asked now, and she was aware of his brown hand on the coverlet, only inches from her ankle. Had those hands picked her up and carried her into the bedroom? she wondered. Somehow she couldn't see Perry lifting her up off the floor.

'I'm fine,' she answered at last, pushing back her hair with a nervous hand. 'Honestly I am. I don't know why I fainted like that. It's never happened before.'

'I guess it was something of a shock to see me,' Matthew offered, his lips twisting sardonically. 'Particularly as I interrupted you. What exactly were you doing?' he asked mildly.

Olivia gasped. 'I beg your pardon?' she exclaimed, as a belated awareness of the significance of Matthew's being here assaulted her. Until now, she had been having a hard time believing that he had been civil to Perry. But suddenly, the consequence of his having crossed the Atlantic to see her reminded her of the reasons why he shouldn't be here, and she clasped her hands uneasily.

'I said——' he began again, but Olivia moved her head back and forth in an agitated gesture.

'I—I know what you said,' she got out unsteadily. 'But—you have no right to ask me. And—and no right to send Perry away either. This—this isn't Lower Mychett, Matt. This is New York.'

'I know where it is,' Matthew told her, in a rough voice, and then, before she could do anything to save herself, he reached out and grasped her ankle, jerking her down the bed until her head was flat against the coverlet. 'But don't tell me what I can or can't do where you're concerned,' he added, leaning across her to put one hand on either side of her head. 'Right now, I'm in no mood to make the distinction.'

'Matt——' she protested weakly, making a desperate effort to straighten the legs of her culottes once again, but he wasn't listening to her. He was looking into her eyes, and she felt herself drowning in their liquid, sensual depths. And, when he lowered his head to hers, the realisation that she had no real moral need to stop him overrode her will to resist him.

His mouth was hot and hungry, seizing her lips in a burning kiss that defied any lingering inhibitions. And, although he was still supporting himself with his hands, his chest was brushing her breasts, inspiring the need to have him even closer. She moaned, deep in her throat, and then she wound her arms around his neck and pulled him down to her, his weight the final reassurance that this was no dream.

His mouth hardened then, the kiss deepening and lengthening, and his tongue slipped between her teeth. It invaded her mouth possessively, wet and demanding, and when it slid along the length of hers her senses swam. She sank into a dark sea of sensation, without any desire to save herself.

'You want me,' he said huskily, his low, impassioned voice scraping every sensitised nerve in her body, and she lifted one leg to wind it about him.

'Mmm,' she breathed, gripping the hair at his nape to bring his mouth back to hers, and Matthew was not proof against that helpless admission.

His hands slid down her back, urging her body up to his, so that she was made insistently aware of his arousal, and fire sped along her veins, igniting everywhere it touched. Whenever Matthew touched her, it was always like this, she thought achingly, her hands invading the neck of his shirt to stroke the moist skin of his shoulders. His body was so familiar to her, and she split the buttons of his shirt to press her lips to his chest.

'God, Liv,' he groaned, brushing the pleated lapels of her jacket aside to expose the creamy flesh of her throat. 'When I came in here tonight and saw you kissing— kissing—well, I wanted to kill him! I wanted to kill both of you!' He buried his face in the dusky hollow between her breasts, and she felt his tongue against her skin. 'I guess it was just as well you fainted. It brought me to my senses.'

'Oh, Matt!' Olivia didn't feel much like talking at that moment, but she had to explain. 'Perry and I weren't— kissing. Well, not in the way you mean, anyway,' she added, sliding her palms against his cheeks. 'I—I'd just told him I loved someone else——'

'You had?' Now, when Olivia tried to draw him down to her again, Matthew resisted. His eyes darkened. 'Tell me about it.'

Olivia sighed. 'Not now, Matt——'

'Yes, now.' Matthew used his hands again to put some space between them. 'Tell me who this—someone is.'

Olivia groaned. 'You know!'

'Do I?' For a man who had just been given the answer he had previously professed to want, Matthew was acting very strangely, and Olivia stared at him.

'Of course you do,' she exclaimed. 'It's you!'

'Is it?'

He pushed himself up into a sitting position now, and Olivia gazed at him in dismayed confusion. 'What's the matter?' she cried. 'What's wrong? I—I thought that was what you wanted to hear.'

Matthew's mouth compressed. 'Then why did you leave England a second time?' he demanded harshly. 'Come on, Liv. I want to hear.'

Olivia swallowed now and sat up, resting her elbows on her knees and propping her head in her hands. 'You know why,' she said heavily. 'You're married.'

'And that's the only reason?' he questioned grimly, and she nodded.

'What else could there be?' she asked him wearily. 'You know I love you. There's never been any doubt of that.'

'Hasn't there?' Matthew gripped her shoulders now, shaking her, so that her head tipped back on the slender column of her neck, and she looked at him uncomprehendingly.

'No.'

'Then why did you leave me ten years ago?' he grated. 'I wasn't married then.'

'Oh——' Olivia's head sagged forward again, and she felt the sharp brush of tears behind her eyes, as he let her go. For a few moments there, she had allowed herself to forget the past, but she should have known better. The past was all bound up with the present, and she couldn't ignore either. But, for a brief spell, she had escaped, and now she had to face the consequences. 'I had my reasons.'

'What reasons?'

Matthew was persistent, and she couldn't honestly blame him. But it was not her story to tell. It never had been. And what was the point of raking it all up now, when Helen still stood between them?

'It's a long story,' she said, as she had said to Perry earlier. 'It doesn't concern us. And I'd rather not go into it.'

'And if I want to?' he insisted, and her eyes encountered his in wary protest.

'Why should you?' she cried. 'It doesn't alter the situation. You are still married——' A desperate thought occurred to her. 'Aren't you?' But her hopes were dashed by his barely perceptible nod. 'We can't change what happened now. It's—too late.'

'Maybe not.' Matthew's words were low, but she heard them, and her head jerked up again.

'What do you mean?'

'I mean it might not be too late for us,' said Matthew quietly, and she stared at him in disbelief.

CHAPTER FIFTEEN

'But—Helen! The stables——'

'The stables have gone,' said Matthew, without emphasis. 'They burned down over two weeks ago. It was quite an inferno. Several horses were killed.'

Olivia was staggered. 'I can't believe it.'

'Nevertheless, it's true.'

Olivia shook her head. 'But how—I mean—did you——?'

'I had nothing to do with it,' exclaimed Matthew indignantly. 'Christ, what an opinion you have of me!'

'I didn't mean that.' Olivia didn't really know what she meant. Her mind was too busy, buzzing with all the possibilities this might create, but for the moment, she had to be pragmatic. 'Helen didn't——?'

'Helen's fine,' said Matthew flatly, and Olivia felt a reluctant sense of relief. Although the other woman's death would have given Matthew his freedom, that was not the way she would have wished it to be.

'So—how——?'

Matthew shrugged. 'It was arson,' he said flatly.

'Arson? But who——?'

'The police think it was Helen,' he replied without expression, and Olivia caught her breath.

'Surely they must be wrong?'

'I don't think so.' Matthew paused, and then went on, 'It wasn't a very professional job, you see. As far as anyone can gather, it was started in the disused barn, adjoining the stables, and it's pretty obvious it wasn't intended to destroy the animals. Helen would never have done anything that might hurt her horses. But it all got out of hand.'

Olivia shook her head. 'But why would she do it?'

'Why do you think? For the insurance money, of course. Although anyone else would have realised that the insurance company were going to find two hefty claims from the same individual pretty hard to stomach.' He sighed. 'But Helen was never entirely rational when it came to her horses, and I suppose she was desperate.'

Olivia frowned. 'But she must have intended to get the horses out.'

'Oh, yes. That would have been her intention. But old Ben Taylor, who was a kind of odd job man around the place, had bought some creosote the day before, and he'd left it in the barn overnight.'

'My God!'

'Yes.' Matthew acknowledged her horror. 'It was pretty terrible. The place went up like a Roman candle, and if we hadn't held Helen back she'd have died with her horses.'

Olivia didn't know what to say now, except, 'I—I'm sorry.'

'For Helen?' Matthew arched his dark brows. 'Yes. So am I, I guess. Although I have to say I'm not sorry to see the back of the Berrenger Stables.'

'But—what about the other horses?'

'They've all had to be sold to help pay off the mortgage. Thankfully, my father's insurance company didn't hold him in any way responsible. He's only left with the mortgage on Rycroft.'

Olivia frowned. 'But Helen isn't—isn't in prison, is she?'

'Oh, no.' For the first time, the trace of a smile touched Matthew's lips. 'My father prevailed upon a lawyer friend of his to act on her behalf, and he thinks it's possible she may get away with a heavy fine. Who knows? In any event, she's left the village. She said she couldn't bear to live there any more, now the stables have gone.'

Olivia swallowed. 'So—does that mean——?' She couldn't say the words, but Matthew said them for her.

'That we're getting a divorce?' He regarded her with cool assessing eyes. 'Yes. I guess it does.'

'Oh, Matthew!'

Olivia could hardly believe it was true. But she wanted to. So much. Without hesitation, she launched herself at Matthew, wrapping her arms around his neck, and burying her face in his shoulder. She was laughing and crying, all at the same time, and it took her several minutes to realise that Matthew wasn't sharing her excitement.

When it did eventually dawn on her that he had made no move to touch her, was not responding in any way at all to her eager advances, an unpleasant chill invaded her stomach. Surely there was nothing wrong now, she thought apprehensively. She'd told him she loved him, so what more did he want?

'M-Matt?' she stammered, drawing back a short way, so that she could look into his face, and he met her anxious gaze unsmilingly. 'Matt, what is it? What's wrong? Why are you looking at me like that? Don't— don't you want us to be together?'

Matthew's hands came up then and gripped her arms, forcing them down to her sides. But although his action sent a wave of anguish through her heart, his words were not what she had expected to hear.

'Don't—talk—rubbish!' he told her savagely, and even though he was hurting her the pain was worth the passion in his voice. 'It's what I've always wanted, God knows,' he continued, gazing at her with grim repression. 'But until I know why you left me years ago I'll never have a moment's peace, whatever your mother says.'

Olivia blinked. 'What—whatever my mother says?' she echoed faintly. 'What did my mother say?'

'Never mind that now——'

'No, I mean it.' Olivia fought free of his restraining hands to gaze anxiously at him. 'Tell me: what did my mother say? It might be important.'

'The same way it was important for me to know why you walked out on me?' ground out Matthew violently, and she groaned.

'Darling, I know that's important to you,' she exclaimed, and, with more confidence than she had had moments before, she brushed her lips against his. 'But, I promise I'll tell you everything,' she went on, even though his response to her eager lips had been more than she could have hoped. 'Just tell me what my mother told you. I really need to know.'

Matthew stared at her for a long time, and then, as if unable to prevent himself, he pulled her into his arms. 'It had better be good,' he said hoarsely, and she could hear the taut emotion in his voice. 'All right,' he went on, forcing himself to speak coherently, even though she sensed his raw frustration. 'She said I should come after you. She said she was sure you did still care about me, and that I should tell you that she'd remembered another letter, that had been with the ones she showed you.' He frowned. 'Does that make sense?'

Olivia drew back. 'She said *that*?'

'Mmm.' Matthew's hands curved around her throat, and he tipped her face up to his. 'So go on, tell me what it means. I think I deserve to know.'

Olivia's tongue came to moisten her lips, and she took a few moments to absorb what Matthew had said. There had been only one significant difference between the letters they had found in her grandmother's box, and that was the fact that one of the letters had been from her mother to Matthew's father, and not the other way about. Which meant . . .

Olivia trembled. 'My—my mother is all right, isn't she?'

'When I last saw her,' conceded Matthew tersely. 'Liv, if this is some ploy to——'

'It's not.' But Olivia had to marshal her thoughts. If her mother had remembered that other letter, did that mean she had guessed what had happened after all?

'Liv——'

'All right, all right.' Olivia took a deep breath. 'My—my mother—knew—your father—years ago. Before I was born.'

'Knew—as in the Biblical sense, I suppose you mean,' remarked Matthew drily. But he didn't sound surprised, and Olivia was disturbed.

'Why—why, yes,' she said unevenly. 'Did you know?'

'I thought everyone knew that old story,' replied Matthew wearily. 'What has that to do with us? Surely it was no reason to break up our relationship!'

'Well, no.' But Olivia sounded as disconcerted as she felt, and Matthew gave an impatient shake of his head.

'Christ, that wasn't the reason, was——?'

'*No!*' She had to silence him, and she did, but once again it took her a few minutes to regain her composure. 'You don't understand, I—my grandmother showed me some letters. Letters written by your father to my mother.'

Matthew's mouth twisted. 'My God! How the hell did she get hold of them?'

'I'm not sure. I think she must have found them when my mother threw them away, and kept them. Goodness knows why.'

'Even so——'

'There's more,' said Olivia tensely. 'There—there was another letter, with your father's letters. A letter my mother had written to your father, but never sent.' She paused, and then plunged on, 'It was to tell him she was pregnant. My grandmother said *I* was the result.'

Matthew   blinked   now.   'You   mean—you thought——'

'—that you were my half-brother, yes.' Olivia caught her breath. 'Now, do you see why I had to go away? I couldn't—we couldn't—there was no way I could tell you that.'

'Oh, Christ!'

Matthew continued to stare at her as she explained the rest. How Harriet Stoner had told her that even her father—her mother's husband, that was—didn't know she wasn't his daughter, nor Matthew's father either. That her mother thought it was her secret, but that her grandmother, being a God-fearing woman, could not let their relationship continue.

'So, you see,' Olivia finished, 'I had to go away. I knew if I stayed in the village it would be much much worse. And who knows? I might have given in, if you'd continued to want me. Where you're concerned, my resistance is very low.'

Matthew groaned. 'You could have fooled me!'

'Oh, Matt!' She wound her arms around his neck. 'You do forgive me, don't you?'

By way of an answer, Matthew bore her back against the pillows, and the urgent pressure of his mouth on hers was all the proof she needed. For the first time in years, she could return his kiss without restraint, and the tenor of his breathing revealed his own response.

'I should strangle you, you know,' he said, unbuttoning her jacket, and exposing the lacy bra beneath. 'You should have realised that affair was over long before you were born. Your mother was only a kid at the time. My mother told me that.'

'She did?' Olivia convulsed as his thumb probed the lacy trim of the bra and found her hardened nipple. 'Well—I——' She caught her breath. 'I was just a kid when Gran told me. She—she must have made a mistake.'

'Like hell,' growled Matthew, lifting his head and scowling at her. 'I guess that other old story about your grandmother having a thing for my grandfather isn't just gossip after all. You must have been her means of revenging herself on the Ryan family.'

Olivia's fingers curled into his hair. 'What are you talking about?'

'Well, it's old gossip,' he admitted, his gaze dropping to her mouth, and her hands slid down his chest. 'According to my mother, old Harriet had no love for the Ryans after my grandfather married someone else.' He shook his head. 'It's ironic really. That three generations of our families should have shared a common bond. And if your grandmother had had her way the result would have been the same.'

Olivia moved her head helplessly from side to side. 'I never knew.'

'No—well, it is history,' murmured Matthew, drawing her hands back to his body. 'Unfasten my shirt, will you? I think I'm overdressed.'

Olivia did so with trembling fingers, but she was still shaking her head. 'I had no idea,' she whispered. 'Oh, God! How could she?'

'We'll never know,' said Matthew softly, and, realising he had to divert her, he added, 'So tell me, when did you find out it wasn't true? About our being related, I mean. And why didn't you tell me then?'

'Oh——' Olivia spread her palms against the fine hair that covered his chest. 'My mother told me. Indirectly, of course. We—we were going through Gran's things, and we found the letters, you see. She—she told me the whole story. About her miscarrying the baby, and your mother getting pregnant with you, all at the same time. She didn't know I'd seen them before, and I couldn't tell her.'

'No?'

'No.' Olivia sighed. 'She's not strong, as you know, and I was afraid that if I approached her with what Gran had told me she might blame herself. I—I couldn't allow that.'

'Oh, Liv!'

'I even took the letters from her, before she could see the letter she had written to your father, telling him about the baby.'

'The *other* letter,' said Matthew, with sudden illumination. 'So—do you think she knows now?'

'Maybe. Maybe she put two and two together and made four,' agreed Olivia huskily. 'Oh, Matt! I'm so glad she did. You might not have come otherwise.'

'I wouldn't bet on it,' muttered Matthew ruefully. 'As I've said before, I don't seem able to stay away from you.'

She cradled his face between her hands. 'Thank God!'

'But that still doesn't explain why you didn't tell me three weeks ago,' he reminded her.

'I wanted to.' Olivia remembered how much. 'But I couldn't stand by and let you sell the estate—not just for me.'

'You mean Helen's ultimatum, don't you?' he said heavily, and she nodded. 'You knew I'd do it, didn't you?'

'I—thought you might,' she admitted softly. 'But I couldn't take that responsibility. Not when you might have hated me for it later.'

'Hated you?' Matthew's mouth twitched. 'God, you don't now how often I've wished I could hate you. Particularly when you refused to marry me. I think I did hate you then. The trouble was, it didn't last.'

'Oh, Matt!'

The kiss that followed was taut with unfulfilled longing, and she eased his shirt off his shoulders, so that her hands could move over the smooth silky skin of his back. But when her hands went to his belt the memories overwhelmed her.

'Do you remember the first time I tried to undress you?' she whispered, as the buckle came apart in her hands. 'I didn't know what to expect then.'

'Well, you do now,' said Matthew thickly, responding to her sensual caress. 'God, Liv—don't do that! Not until I've got my pants off anyway...'

Hours later, Olivia stirred, roused by Matthew sliding off the bed and striding across the floor. 'Where are you going?' she protested sleepily, switching on the lamp so that she could admire his lean, muscled body. 'It's hours yet till morning.'

'I need a drink,' Matthew told her drily, heading for the kitchen. 'You may be used to drinking champagne, but I'm not.'

'Oh.'

Olivia smiled lazily, and rolled over on to her back. Indeed, she didn't seem to be able to stop smiling, and Matthew pulled a face at her before disappearing out the door. But they had drunk a whole magnum of champagne, in between periods of making love, and Olivia felt both pleasantly relaxed and slightly intoxicated. But it was Matthew who had intoxicated her, not the champagne, and although she ached a little it was a most delightful feeling.

But the best part of all was knowing that when he went back to England she would be going with him. Agnes could continue running the agency, and now she might seriously consider setting up one in England. But that was for the future. Right now, making Matthew happy was the most important thing.

As for her mother, she guessed that one day soon she would tell her the truth. If she hadn't already guessed it, of course. Evidently Felicity Stoner was stronger than any of them had given her credit for being. Even her grandmother, Olivia reflected ruefully.

Matthew came back, drinking a glass of water, and as he approached the bed Olivia's eyes drifted down over his body. There was a singular delight in just looking at him, in knowing she had the right to do so, and Matthew was not indifferent to the possessive gleam in her eyes.

Even so, he finished the water in his glass before joining her on the bed, and Olivia eyed him teasingly as he stretched his length beside her.

'You have no modesty, do you?' she exclaimed, stroking her fingernail along the hair-roughened skin of his thigh, and he shifted restlessly.

'Nor do you,' he told her, turning to imprison her beneath him. His heavy arousal throbbed against her leg, and she rubbed herself against him eagerly.

'You never did tell me how you got in here,' she remembered, some time later, and Matthew eased himself away from her reluctantly.

'I told the doorman I was your brother, and I wanted to surprise you,' admitted Matthew ruefully. 'An unfortunate choice of relationship in the circumstances, but I guess, as I was English, too, he believed me.'

'Thank goodness he did,' murmured Olivia huskily, winding her arms around his neck. 'But I'll tell him the truth tomorrow. That's one mistake I never want to make again.'

BARBARY WHARF

An exciting six-book series, one title per month
beginning in October, by bestselling author

Set in the glamorous and fast-paced world of international
journalism, BARBARY WHARF will take you from the
Sentinel's hectic newsroom to the most thrilling cities in the
world. You'll meet media tycoon Nick Caspian and his
adversary Gina Tyrrell, whose dramatic story of passion and
heartache develops throughout the six-book series.

In book one, BESIEGED (#1498), you'll also meet Hazel and
Piet. Hazel's always had a good word to say about everyone.
Well, almost. She just can't stand Piet Van Leyden, Nick's
chief architect and one of the most arrogant know-it-alls she's
ever met! As far as Hazel's concerned, Piet's a twentieth-
century warrior, and she's the one being besieged!

Don't miss the sparks in the first BARBARY WHARF
book, BESIEGED (#1498), available in October from
Harlequin Presents.

BARB-S

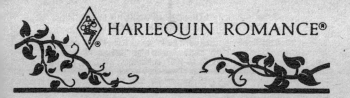

HARLEQUIN ROMANCE®

**Harlequin Romance
knows love can be dangerous!**

Don't miss
TO LOVE AND PROTECT (#3223)
by Kate Denton,
the October title in

THE BRIDAL COLLECTION

THE GROOM'S life was in peril.
THE BRIDE was hired to help him.
BUT THEIR WEDDING was *more* than
a business arrangement!

Available this month in
The Bridal Collection
JACK OF HEARTS (#3218)
by Heather Allison
Wherever Harlequin books are sold.